SiXTY-EiGHT
4 ROOMS
··THE SECRET OF THE KEY··

ALSO BY MARIANNE MALONE

1 · *The Sixty-Eight Rooms*
2 · *Stealing Magic*
3 · *The Pirate's Coin*

SIXTY-EIGHT ROOMS

4 ROOMS

··THE SECRET OF THE KEY··

. . .

MARIANNE MALONE
ILLUSTRATIONS BY GREG CALL

A YEARLING BOOK

Text copyright © 2014 by Marianne Malone
Cover art and interior illustrations copyright © 2014 by Greg Call

All rights reserved. Published in the United States by Yearling, an imprint of Random House Children's Books, a division of Penguin Random House LLC, New York.

Originally published in hardcover in the United States by Random House Children's Books, New York, in 2014.

Yearling and the jumping horse design are registered trademarks of Penguin Random House LLC.

Photograph credits: © The Art Institute of Chicago. Mrs. James Ward Thorne, American, 1882–1966, E4: English Drawing Room of the Late Jacobean Period, 1680–1702, c. 1937, Miniature room, mixed media, Interior: 16 3/4 x 26 1/2 x 21 5/8 in., Gift of Mrs. James Ward Thorne, 1941.1189, The Art Institute of Chicago (p. 232); © ClassicStock/Alamy (p. 234); Library of Congress, Prints & Photographs Division [LC-DIG-matpc-23053] (p. 235)

Visit us on the Web! randomhousekids.com

Educators and librarians, for a variety of teaching tools, visit us at RHTeachersLibrarians.com

The Library of Congress has cataloged the hardcover edition of this work as follows:
Malone, Marianne.
The secret of the key : a Sixty-eight rooms adventure / Marianne Malone ; illustrations by Greg Call. — First edition.
pages cm.
Sequel to: The pirate's coin.
Summary: In the Art Institute of Chicago's miniature Thorne Rooms, the Thorne Rooms key and a mysterious set of rings lead Ruthie and Jack to new historical eras and a woman who went missing as a young girl.
ISBN 978-0-307-97721-2 (trade) — ISBN 978-0-307-97723-6 (ebook)
1. Art Institute of Chicago—Juvenile fiction. [1. Art Institute of Chicago—Fiction. 2. Time travel—Fiction. 3. Miniature rooms—Fiction. 4. Size—Fiction. 5. Magic—Fiction.] I. Call, Greg, illustrator. II. Title.
PZ7.M29646Se 2014 [Fic]—dc23 2013028270

ISBN 978-0-307-97724-3 (pbk.)

Printed in the United States of America

First Yearling Edition 2015

Random House Children's Books supports the First Amendment and celebrates the right to read.

FOR THE NEIGHBORHOOD KIDS
OF THE STATE STREETS,
Urbana, Illinois, 1984–2003

···CONTENTS···

1. The Ring Dial 1
2. The Hourglass. 11
3. Freddy 18
4. Not New Hampshire 30
5. New York, New York 45
6. The Wooden Box 62
7. One Clue Closer 74
8. The Other Way In 84
9. The Governess. 95
10. Hints 107
11. Telling Stories 122
12. Slippery Stones 135
13. A Reason to Lie. 149
14. A Sticky Spot 160
15. Fugitives. 170
16. The Choice 180
17. Montjoie. 193
18. Hope of Future Years 205
19. The Spell 219
    Author's Note 233
    Resources. 237
    Acknowledgments. 239

THE RING DIAL

A JOB—A REAL JOB! Ruthie Stewart repeated to herself. Heat radiated up from the sidewalk even though it was only ten-thirty in the morning, but she barely noticed.

"Hey, slow down, kiddo," her dad called. He was walking her to Mrs. McVittie's Rare and Antique Bookshop. "Did you even hear a word I was saying?"

She didn't. Ruthie turned, waiting for her dad to catch up. It's just that she had never had a job before, and now Mrs. McVittie had asked her and Jack to help out in the shop this summer. She could use extra hands for opening boxes, sorting, and dusting.

At the start of every summer, Ruthie thought only of glorious days filled with nothing but free time ahead. Boredom? Impossible. But school had been out for a couple of weeks. Jack had signed up for Chinese lessons, and he had piano too. Her parents were busy teaching summer school, and her sister, Claire, would be going away on a summer-abroad program. Ruthie's schedule was open until she went off to camp in August, and the reality of having nothing to do had begun creeping into her thoughts like an annoying fly in the room.

Of course, what she *really* wanted to do with her time was explore the magical Thorne Rooms at the Art Institute, the sixty-eight miniature time portals that beckoned her with their promise of trips to past worlds. But she couldn't spend every day in the museum, not without raising her parents' suspicion.

"What I was saying," her dad repeated pointedly, "is that it's supposed to reach over ninety degrees today. I want you and Jack to make sure Minerva keeps the AC on."

"We will, Dad," she promised.

They arrived at the shop, the Closed sign still in place. Ruthie pressed the doorbell.

"Good morning," Mrs. McVittie said when she let them in. "Jack's already here—I've got him started in the back."

"Bye, Dad," Ruthie said.

Ruthie loved Mrs. McVittie's shop. It was long and narrow, lined floor to ceiling with sagging shelves of old leather-bound books. Antiques were scattered here and there, along with silver pieces, like boxes and candlesticks, and more than a few small, framed oil paintings. And Mrs. McVittie was constantly adding and changing things, so it was always different. The smell of the shop was a distinctive mix of dust and leather, with all the scents the old things had picked up over their lifetimes, in some cases a century or more. Sometimes Ruthie marveled at the thought of where all these things had been.

Ruthie headed to the storeroom at the far end of the shop. It was a windowless space except for a skylight high above, and was crammed with years' worth of inventory collected from estate sales and auctions. Her best friend was nowhere to be seen.

Deep in the room, down a narrow pathway formed between high piles of boxes and packing crates, she finally found him sitting cross-legged on the floor. There was an opened box next to him, and he was reading a yellowed newspaper.

"Hi," Jack said without looking up.

"When did you get here?" Ruthie asked.

"'Bout a half hour ago. Man, Watergate was really something."

"What?"

"Watergate. The big scandal that made President Nixon resign." Jack held up a crumpled but now smoothed-out old newspaper. "See? Nineteen seventy-four!"

Ruthie read the headline, in bold two-inch-high letters: "Nixon Resigns."

"And look at this one from 1980." Jack held up another that read, "Beatle John Lennon Slain."

"You're reading old newspapers?" Ruthie asked.

"All this stuff we're supposed to unpack is wrapped in them. It's pretty cool. I'm saving some."

Jack loved history. This was going to slow him down for sure, Ruthie thought.

"Yeah, but what are we supposed to be doing with the stuff *inside* the newspapers?"

"Oh, right," Jack said, and looked up. "There's a clipboard for you on the shelf over there. Mrs. McVittie wants us to write down a description of everything. There are directions on your clipboard."

"Okay. Sounds easy."

Ruthie retrieved the clipboard that Mrs. McVittie had set out for her and chose a box to start with. This one was filled with books. She carefully followed the directions, jotting down as much information as she could.

They worked through the morning, and Mrs. McVittie came to check on their progress from time to time. At noon she ordered sandwiches from a local deli and they sat together in the front room.

"Not too dull, I hope?" Mrs. McVittie asked them.

"It's better than doing nothing at home," Ruthie said, munching a dill pickle.

"I think it's interesting—there's so much to read about," Jack added.

After lunch they went back to work. Ruthie was amazed at how much was in the storeroom. She worked faster than Jack, it was true, but he kept them entertained with his running monologue about any article that piqued his interest. He read about current events, politics, robberies, and other crimes that had occurred in the city.

As she unwrapped a plate, a rumpled newsprint image caught Ruthie's eye. "This must have been great."

She held up a full-page ad from 1977 for an exhibition at the Field Museum called the Treasures of Tutankhamun. Surrounded by his impressive headdress, King Tut, the boy pharaoh of Egypt, stared out from the newspaper with his kohl-rimmed eyes.

"Cool!" Jack responded. "I'll save that one too."

As Jack looked at the page, Ruthie saw a headline on the other side: "Missing Teen Case Unsolved." She skimmed the article about a girl named Becky Brown who had been babysitting her little brother and vanished without a trace. It gave Ruthie chills to think how that could happen to someone.

"Ruthie," Mrs. McVittie said, entering the room and walking over to a sturdy-looking container, "could I ask you to open this crate next? I'm looking for something that came from a particular estate sale."

"Sure." Ruthie handed the newspaper with the King Tut ad to Jack. "What should I be on the lookout for?"

"Anything eighteenth-century, preferably English. I have a client interested in things from the latter half of that century," Mrs. McVittie answered, and went back into the shop, but not before looking askance at Jack's sparsely filled-in clipboard.

The crate Mrs. McVittie had asked Ruthie to unpack was mostly filled with household objects: some fragile-looking porcelain, a silver dish, a few delicately embroidered handkerchiefs, and a small wooden box, a cube of about eight inches. It was made of fine wood with hinges on one side and a keyhole on the other. Ruthie tried lifting the lid. *Locked!*

She rummaged through the bottom of the crate, carefully sifting through the last crumpled newsprint packaging. *Aha!* She pulled out a key. It was made of brass and was obviously old, but not very ornate. She held it up for a few seconds to see how the light hit it. A beam of late-afternoon sunshine streamed in from the skylight at a sharp angle.

"What's that?" Jack asked.

"Probably nothing. Just a key."

"*Just* a key?" Since finding the magic one belonging to the sixteenth-century duchess Christina of Milan, neither of them could look at keys in the same way. Especially not old ones! Could this one also have some kind of power?

Jack came over to her and studied the key. "Do you know what it goes to?"

"This, I think." She pointed out the wooden box she had just removed from the crate.

Ruthie tried the key in the keyhole. It fit. She turned it a half turn and they both heard the satisfying metal-on-wood sound of the lock unlatching. She gave Jack a quick grin before opening the box.

Inside, the box was lined with worn crimson velvet. Nestled in the center was a metal object consisting of two flat disk-like rings, one within the other, and a crosspiece. Like the key, it was made of what looked like brass (yellow, but not as shiny as gold). Each ring had markings carved into it: *London 51, Paris 48,* and *Rome 41.* Ruthie lifted it out.

"What is it?" Jack asked.

"I don't know, but whatever it is, it's beautiful," Ruthie said. "It reminds me of a Christmas tree ornament."

"Maybe Mrs. McVittie knows what it is."

They brought it out to the front room, where Mrs. McVittie was sitting at her desk, doing some paperwork. She looked over her reading glasses at them. "Ah. A universal equinoctial ring dial."

"A what?" Ruthie asked.

"It's an eighteenth-century ring dial. It was used to tell time. I believe I have a few back there."

"How does it work?" Jack asked, grabbing a caramel from the crystal dish that Mrs. McVittie always kept on her desk. He unwrapped it and popped it in his mouth.

"It's essentially a sundial, only portable," Mrs. McVittie explained.

"You mean like the things you see in gardens, where the sun casts a shadow that lines up with the hour?" Ruthie asked.

"Yes. First you need to know the date." She took the dial and slid a movable sleeve—which had a tiny hole in it—along the crosspiece. "These are the letters of the months etched here, with markings for the days." She set it for today's date. "Then the latitude."

"Oh, I get it," Jack said.

"Let's see—Chicago is roughly latitude forty-one degrees north. The smaller ring is calibrated with hours etched into it." She swiveled the rings into place, rose from her chair, and went to the window at the front of the shop. Holding the dial from a silk cord attached to the top of the outer ring, she let the sun shine on it.

The three watched for a moment as the ring dial swayed and twirled. Finally a beam of sunlight pierced through the tiny hole, hitting the hour ring.

"Half past three," Mrs. McVittie declared.

Jack checked his watch. "That's right!"

"These were used by sailors and other travelers," Mrs. McVittie explained. "If used correctly, the outer ring is aligned in a north-south direction, the inner ring is parallel to the equator, and the crosspiece should be parallel to the earth's axis. So it gives you lots of information. Very handy indeed."

Ruthie was intrigued. It was such a simple, compact object, yet it could do so much. "Like an early GPS. And it doesn't need batteries."

Mrs. McVittie put it in Ruthie's hand. It was heavier than it looked. Ruthie's fingers traced the tarnished surface, where the scientific markings were punctuated by decorative flourishes, like flowers and vines.

"Would you like to have it?" Mrs. McVittie offered.

"But it must be valuable," Ruthie replied.

"Oh, not terribly. Maybe it could be part of your payment this week."

Ruthie did some quick mental calculating. This job was going to go on for at least two months. She could spare some cash. "Sure!" she agreed.

Ruthie lay in bed that night thinking about the vast collection of old books and objects that Mrs. McVittie had acquired, not to keep them, but to find new owners for them. She always said she wanted to connect the right things with the right people. The librarian at her school did something similar, making sure all the kids found exactly the right books to read. But Minerva McVittie was dealing with things that were often fragile or valuable and had layers of histories. Like the ring dial.

Ruthie pictured it again, dangling in front of the shop window. She imagined who might have carried it long ago; a sailor navigating across the ocean on a dangerous voyage of exploration in a creaking wooden ship. Maybe Jack's pirate ancestor, Jack Norfleet, relied on one. Or perhaps someone like Sophie Lacombe, the young woman they'd met from revolutionary France who traveled abroad with her husband—she might have needed a portable timepiece.

The lives of the people she'd met through the Thorne Rooms were filled with the kind of adventure that Ruthie yearned for. Claire, snoring in the bed next to her, would be going off on her own study-abroad trip soon. Ruthie fell asleep despite the inkling of an urge, which would grow overnight into an obsession; she couldn't exactly take off and travel, but as long as she had the magic key, she could *explore*.

THE HOURGLASS

DECIDING WHICH ROOM OF THE sixty-eight miniatures they should visit first, Ruthie stopped in front of room E9, a beautiful drawing room. It was Thursday morning and Mrs. McVittie had given them the day off because she had appointments. Jack's mom had invited Ruthie to come for dinner with Edmund Bell and his daughter, Dr. Caroline Bell. She and Jack had the entire day to explore.

"This one is copied from a house in England around 1730," she called over to Jack.

"It's okay—kind of fancy, though." He was already moving to the next window.

"Hey, look." Ruthie pointed at something through the glass.

Jack came back. "What?"

"See that hourglass on the table in the back?" Jack nodded. "It doesn't belong in this room; it's not in the catalogue,"

Ruthie said, referring to the book that included photographs of all sixty-eight rooms—a book she knew by heart.

"Let's check it out."

They moved directly to the alcove and the door that led to the access corridor behind the rooms.

"Ready?" Jack said in a low voice.

Ruthie glanced around the gallery. No one was looking. "Ready."

Jack sandwiched Duchess Christina's magic key between their hands. Its warmth penetrated all the way to Ruthie's fingertips and sent a small, tingling shock wave through her. An otherworldly breeze blew, wrapping around them, and the space of the alcove stretched and expanded. Ruthie felt the size of her body decreasing. Their clothing readjusted as they shrank, getting smaller and smaller with each second. When the process stopped, they stood five inches tall, directly in front of the now shin-high crack under the alcove door. Ruthie let go of Jack's hand and they rolled under the door and into the dark corridor behind the European rooms.

"How many times do you think we've done this now?" Jack mused, as he came to his feet.

"I don't know—dozens at least."

"It's still awesome."

They made the trek up Jack's handmade toothpick ladder to the ledge that ran along the back of all the rooms. The tiny duo navigated through the wooden framework supporting the displays until they found a set of tall double doors that opened into the rear of room E9. The doors were ajar, which made going in so much easier; they could take a peek first. The museum wasn't very busy, and they were able to walk in.

Magic was at work. Light streamed through the two tall windows. It felt like sunshine, not electric light, a distinction hard to describe, but Ruthie had discovered that it was a sensation notably different than warmth from lightbulbs. They heard the sound of birds chirping outside and the room smelled old, of leather and books and sunlight on wood.

"I wonder what the animator is," Ruthie said, referring to the antique object that turned the miniature rooms and the painted dioramas outside of them into portals—passages to the real, live worlds of the past. A closed door on the far wall led to one of these worlds.

"Could be anything—a statue, a book, one of those candlesticks." Jack nodded to the set on the mantel.

The walls were painted creamy white and the high, vaulted ceiling was decorated with an all-over pattern of carved octagons. A bookcase filled with colorful bound volumes stood at the back of the room. Gold and blue silk covered the chairs, and a landscape painting hung above the fireplace. Urns and vases, some small statuettes, and a grand crystal chandelier decorated the room.

"Here's the hourglass," Ruthie said, walking over to a round table. It was the kind of hourglass with sand that pours from the top through the narrow middle to the bottom. It had a wood top and base. "It looks . . . off."

"What do you mean, *off*?"

"It's a little too rough. Everything else in this room is really well made."

They heard voices nearby in the gallery. Jack ducked behind a curtain, Ruthie behind a sofa. They waited, listening.

When the viewers had moved on, Jack came over to Ruthie.

"I think this was made as a miniature, not magically shrunk," she said. They had discovered that a surprising number of objects not made by Mrs. Thorne or her craftsmen had found their way—somehow—into the rooms.

"Why not?"

"The grains of sand look too big. They're almost pea size."

"Hmm, yeah, I see what you mean."

Ruthie turned it over to look at the bottom, the way Mrs. McVittie had taught her, hoping to find a signature or some other kind of marking. The chunky sand poured none too smoothly through the narrow middle. She squinted at some smudged and faded ink.

" 'New Hampshire/E.K.' I'm not positive, but I bet E.K. is Eugene Kupjack, one of Mrs. Thorne's master craftsmen. He might have marked it so he'd know where to put it. I remember seeing an hourglass in one of the New Hampshire rooms—A2, I think."

"Maybe the museum people put it in here by mistake."

"Could've been anyone," Ruthie added. "We know more people than us have been in the rooms."

"Let's return it to the New Hampshire room later. After we explore," Jack suggested, tipping his head toward the closed door to the outside.

Ruthie put the hourglass carefully into her messenger bag. "I brought this," she said, and pulled the ring dial out, holding it in her open palm. The sight of it reminded her of why they had come to the museum today. "I want to see if it works."

"Good idea." Jack turned the stiff knob and pulled the door open. He stepped out, leaving Chicago and the twenty-first century behind. Ruthie followed. They stood on a slate patio in the shade of some tall trees in eighteenth-century England.

Crossing the threshold, she felt a tiny burst of heat and a slight flutter in her hand. The sensation was coming from the ring dial. Before her eyes the scuffs and tarnish on the surface melted away and the brass underneath reflected the sunlight like a golden jewel. "Did you see what I just saw?"

"Cool!" Jack exclaimed.

"I guess it makes sense. We're in the time period when the dial was made, so it's brand-new out here."

They had never seen this happen before because they had never brought antiques like this into the past. What they had learned was that it was impossible to bring things from the past worlds into the present. When they had tried, the objects vanished before their eyes. (What they had also discovered was that Mrs. Thorne had put a few true antiques in the rooms, things like those they might find in Mrs. McVittie's shop. Some were antique miniatures—but *some* had been magically shrunken!) Ruthie put the ring dial back in her bag.

The day was bright and warm as they walked away from the door and farther out onto the patio, which was surrounded by a garden. The air smelled fresh and green and was scented with the wild roses that grew along the roadside beyond the garden, very different from Chicago with its bus fumes and Lake Michigan breezes. They had learned that the areas immediately outside the rooms were part of the magic, invisible to the people of the past. As long as they stayed on the patio, they could not be seen by anyone who happened to pass by.

"Too bad we don't have the right clothes," Ruthie said.

"We're only going to look around. We don't have to talk to people," Jack said, but he took off his hefty wristwatch. "This would be hard to explain, though, if we bump into anyone." He slipped it in one of his pockets. "Where do you want to go first?"

The portal seemed to be at the edge of a small village. "How about there?" Ruthie pointed to the left, away from the town.

The road meandered past a few houses, made of stone with thatched roofs, and some other structures clustered near them, and then on into the quiet countryside. It seemed like farmland, of sorts, but not the kind that Ruthie and Jack were used to seeing outside of Chicago, with row upon endless row of corn or soybeans. Here, hedgerows divided the properties into cultivated areas and grassy meadows where sheep and cows grazed. Wooded areas punctuated the landscape, making a patchwork of small, uneven shapes and textures.

Not too far down the road, they came to a church, its steeple cutting the air as it came to a point. As they approached, they saw that the church was bordered by a stone wall enclosing a small graveyard. They counted about thirty simple headstones.

"These are really old!" Jack observed. Many of the stones were weathered and eroded, but they saw that some had sixteenth- or seventeenth-century dates chiseled in them.

"Any idea where in England we might be?"

"The catalogue said Mrs. Thorne based the room on one in a house in a place called Buckinghamshire."

They came to an intersection. To the right, in the distance, they saw what they would call a castle. It was a large stone building and had a center turret with a crenellated top. It sat in the middle of a broad grassy area, high on a hill.

Straight ahead, the road angled downhill and ended at a clear blue lake, just visible through the trees.

"The castle, right?" Jack asked.

"Of course!" Ruthie answered.

···3···
FREDDY

THEY HAD TAKEN A DOZEN or so steps when they heard a crashing rumble coming from behind them and getting louder—fast. Ruthie and Jack spun around and saw a horse-drawn carriage heading in their direction. The sound of horseshoes clomping on gravel and the creaking of the wooden carriage thundered in the peaceful countryside. The vehicle rounded a bend and careened toward them.

Jack grabbed Ruthie's sleeve and yanked her to the side of the road. They ducked behind a tree as the carriage sped by. A young boy sat in the driver's seat, alone.

"Whoa! Whoa!" the boy shrieked, tugging frantically at the reins.

"C'mon!" Ruthie yelled over the sound of the horse whinnying. "He needs help!"

They ran back out onto the road. Even though they were running as fast as they could, the carriage was well ahead.

They were about to give up when it veered to the side, a wheel caught in a rut, and the whole carriage lurched and tilted crazily, nearly toppling over. The boy was thrown from his seat like a rag doll. Also propelled into the air were a water-filled bucket and four glistening fish. The boy and the fish landed in the grass, the flipping fish a contrast to the boy, who lay motionless as Ruthie and Jack raced toward him.

The horse, now without a driver, slowed down and reared before wandering off without regard to what had just happened.

Ruthie knelt down to look at the boy. He was smaller than them, probably a year or two younger. He was breathing, but his eyes were closed and he wasn't moving.

"I'm going to tie up the horse, if I can," Jack said, jogging off to catch the aimless animal.

The boy moaned, shifting his head a little. That was a good sign, Ruthie thought; at least his neck wasn't broken. His hair lay in a lopsided mess of disorderly curls, his white linen shirt torn and grass-stained.

"I tied the horse to a tree over there," Jack said when he came back. "How does he seem?"

"He's moving a little."

"Do you think we should get help?" Jack looked around.

"I think he might be coming to," Ruthie said, noticing the boy's eyelids fluttering.

"Ow . . . where am I?" The boy groaned, reaching up to rub his head. "And who . . . you wouldn't be angels, would you?"

Jack chuckled. "Do we look like angels?"

From the ground, the boy looked them over. "You don't look like you're from here."

"We're not," Jack replied. "We're from the Colonies."

The boy's eyes popped into focus.

"Are you okay?" Ruthie asked.

"Beg pardon?" the boy responded.

That word again! Ruthie reminded herself. Going back in time made her realize how often *okay* rolled off her tongue. "I mean, are you all right?"

"I'm not sure what happened."

"You were thrown from your carriage," Jack explained.

"Oh . . . now I remember. Blossom, she was spooked. A rotten little critter ran 'cross the road and I lost control. You won't be tellin' on me?"

"Aren't you too young to be driving?" Jack asked.

"Who are you to be askin'?" the young boy demanded. "It's me own business."

"We won't tell," Ruthie said. "But let's see if you're hurt. Can you move your arms and legs?"

The boy moved his legs and made small circles with his feet. "They're fine, I'd say." His right arm was fine too. But when he went to move the left, he moaned.

"We can get help," Ruthie said.

"No!" He shook his head and struggled to sit upright. "I can manage."

"Do you live near here?" Jack asked.

With his good arm the boy gestured toward the castle on the hill. "I work at the manor up there."

"What do you do?" Jack asked.

"I work in the stables. Sometimes I help in the scullery." He looked around suddenly. "Me fish!"

"Right here." Jack scrambled to grab the four fish, plunking them back in the bucket. "The water's mostly gone."

"No matter. I can take them straightaway." The boy tried to stand. He wobbled and staggered but made it to his feet.

"You should see a doctor," Jack said.

The boy looked at Jack as though he had landed from another planet. "It'll heal same as a doctor sees it or not!"

"I suppose that's true," Jack responded.

"We'll help you back," Ruthie said. "I'm Ruthie and this is Jack."

"I'm Freddy. Pleased to make your acquaintance." He gave a stiff bow, which caused him to teeter. Jack took Freddy's arm to help him and led him to the carriage.

"I'll lead the horse—you climb on," Jack directed. Ruthie hoisted the bucket with the fish into the back of the carriage.

"Why don't you come aboard?" Freddy said to her.

"Oka . . . all right." Ruthie pulled herself up. It was her first-ever carriage ride and it made her feel like a character in a fairy tale. Jack led the horse slowly along the road but the wooden seat was hard and Freddy winced with each bump in the road.

"Them colonies is wild-like, I hear," Freddy said between bounces.

"It's not too wild," Ruthie answered. "Do you go to school?"

"School?" Freddy looked at her again like she was speaking another language. "Aren't any round here. Anyway, the groom wouldn't like me to be gone from the stable. You?"

Ruthie nodded.

"Do you like it?"

"Yes. But we don't have school in the summer. Jack and I have jobs in a bookstore."

"Books!" He shook his head, his curls bobbing like springs. "Don't have much use for them. But the ladies of the house always have their noses in them."

"Do you like your job?"

"It suits me fine. I have me own bed. And the groom treats me decent, most days." The carriage hit a bigger bump and he groaned in earnest. "I daresay I won't be fishin' for a while."

"You looked worried when Jack asked if you were too young to drive the carriage."

"I went fishin'—I've a secret place—without botherin' to ask. It was early—no one was needin' the carriage." He looked up at the sun. "It's later than I thought. Lost track of the time down at the lake, I did. But they'll be happy 'bout the fish. You'll see."

"What's that?" Ruthie pointed to something in a basket wedged under the seat between them.

"Oh, that? Just me whittlin'."

In the basket Ruthie spied five or six pieces of wood, in various stages of carving, and a sharp knife. "Can I take a look?"

He shrugged, so Ruthie took that as a yes. She picked up one of the more finished pieces. It was a finely carved sculpture of a fish.

She looked further and saw a mouse, a rabbit, and a bird—even a toad. "Did you make all of these?"

"That I did. Just something to pass the time waitin' for the fish to bite."

"These are amazing!" The wooden fish was about six inches long, complete with scales and gills and a tail fin captured in mid-swish. She held it up. "Jack—look at this." Jack stopped the horse and, holding the reins loosely, walked back to the carriage.

"Freddy carved these!" Ruthie tipped the basket so he could see.

Jack pulled the bumpy-skinned toad from the basket; its bulging eyes seemed as though they might blink at him. "You're really good."

Freddy gazed at the sky again. "If you please, could we keep on? I'm in for it now."

Jack returned to the horse and gave it a gentle tug to start it walking again.

"Can't you tell the groom what happened, that your arm is hurt and that's why you're late?"

Freddy shook his head. "Late is late."

His matter-of-fact answer left Ruthie worrying about how serious his punishment would be.

Just before they arrived at the final turn Freddy called down to Jack, "Stop!" Using one hand to steady himself, he managed to climb down before the carriage had come to a full stop. "I'll take it from here."

"Are you sure?" Jack asked, reluctantly handing the reins to him, while Ruthie hopped to the ground.

"I'm going round the back way to the stable. If luck's with me, no one'll be about."

Holding his swollen left arm against his torso, he led the horse away from them. He had gone only a few paces when a gruff voice shouted, "Freddy! What trouble are you makin' for me now?" A stout but muscular man approached, walking with a hulking stride straight toward Freddy. The man had sandy red hair, blue eyes, and crooked brown-stained teeth. "The morning's over and ya haven't started with the stalls yet. How many times is this?"

Freddy shrugged and looked toward the ground.

"And what's happened to ya? Your shirt's torn and smudged! And you've hurt your arm too. That's a fine thing!" He raised his hand as if he were about to slap Freddy but stopped when he noticed Ruthie and Jack, who had been obscured by the body of the horse. "Who might you be?" he growled.

"I'm Jack Tucker and this is Ruthie Stewart."

The man gave them a critical once-over.

"Freddy was thrown back there," Ruthie said. "I think his arm might be broken."

"We'll put a splint to it," the man said. "Serves him right for stealing off and bein' late again."

Jack reached up and grabbed the bucket from the carriage. "He caught these."

The man peered into the bucket, his brow softening in momentary approval.

"Strangers, eh?" the man asked, taking the bucket from Jack with a brusque motion.

"We're visiting from out of town," Ruthie answered.

"From the colonies!" Freddy added.

"It's no business of a stable boy," the man said. He grabbed Freddy by an ear, giving him a yank and a toss toward the stable.

"Ow!" Freddy hollered, and tumbled into a run.

Ruthie approached the man and spoke up. "His arm looks bad."

"I'll see to the boy," the man said, grabbing the reins. He gave them another steely look before leading the horse away, and Ruthie and Jack were left alone.

"Poor guy," Jack said as Freddy disappeared into the stable, the groom close behind.

"I hope he doesn't get in trouble."

"I think he's used to trouble."

"I have an idea," Ruthie said. She opened her messenger bag and lifted the ring dial. "He could really use this to keep track of time. Come on."

Ruthie led the way back to the stable and crept up to a window. They saw the groom ordering Freddy—still favoring his injured arm—to clean out the horse stalls. Soon the man trudged off and out of sight.

Ruthie and Jack tiptoed into the stable. The smell of hay and manure was pungent but oddly fresh. Freddy stepped out from one of the stalls, saw them, and gave a darting look around for the groom.

"We have something for you," Ruthie whispered. She held up the ring dial.

Freddy's eyebrow rose. "What is it?"

"It's called a ring dial," Jack answered. "It will tell you the time—so you won't be late anymore."

"Honest?"

"Come over here." Ruthie stepped back to the doorway, where the sunlight was strong. They gave him a quick lesson on how to use it and watched him do it by himself a few times. He grinned as the dot of sun told him the precise time.

"But I can't take somethin' for nothin'." His smile disappeared and he handed the brass timepiece back to Ruthie.

"It's a gift."

He shook his head, his mouth set.

"We don't need it," Jack insisted.

"I know—how about a trade?" Ruthie suggested. "I'd love to have one of your carvings."

"Doesn't seem like an even trade," Freddy replied.

"It does to me." Ruthie let the ring dial dangle in front of him.

Freddy looked at it. "All right, then." He ran around the corner and came back with the basket of his work. "Choose the one you like."

Knowing what was going to happen when they returned to room E9 made the choice bittersweet. Ruthie took the lively toad in her hand, wanting more than anything to keep it. But she knew there was no chance it would survive passing the threshold back to the twenty-first century.

They said goodbye to Freddy and made their way back to the road.

"That was nice of you to give him the ring dial," Jack said as he and Ruthie approached the door to room E9.

"It's going to be cool to think of someone in the 1700s having something from me!" She held the toad up to look at it one last time, knowing that it would disappear from her hand the moment she reentered room E9. "I really wish I could keep it."

She was about to put her foot in the doorway when Jack grabbed her arm. "Hang on. I have an idea."

"What?"

"Something I just thought of. It probably won't work, but it's worth a try. Wait here."

He ran through the doorway and Ruthie saw him in

the room, looking for something, until he crossed to the right and she couldn't see him anymore.

Then all at once strange things started to happen. The room began to fade. She saw a vague image of him in the distance, walking into view, holding something.

"Jack!" she screamed.

She reached out toward the door but it was slipping off into the distance faster than she could react, moving away from her and getting smaller, shrinking to a tiny dot before disappearing completely. And then the patio and garden around her vanished, replaced by a few trees and rosebushes in front of her and a long rolling landscape beyond. She stood alone on the side of the road, clutching the wooden toad.

NOT NEW HAMPSHIRE

RUTHIE HAD NO IDEA HOW long she stood there, frozen in panic. Calling for help wouldn't work—what could anyone here do for her?

A million thoughts raced through her mind. Jack must have done something to the animator in the room, whatever it was. He would figure it out shortly, she told herself. Surely the door would reappear exactly where it had been moments before. Ruthie kept her eyes on that spot, squinting for any glimpse of the wooden door frame.

She thought she heard the tinkling bell sound that had always signaled that something magic was occurring. But it was only the trill of birds chirping around her, sounding foreign and odd, filtered through her growing anxiety.

Ruthie attempted to breathe deeply and slowly, struggling to keep fear at bay. What if they had changed history somehow, and this was all part of something she didn't understand and couldn't have predicted?

Was that the door appearing? No, it was the smear of tears forming in her eyes, distorting the view in front of her.

Come on, Jack! Get me back!

She checked and saw that the key was still safe in her bag. But could its magic help her? Could it transport her home in some other way?

The clip-clop sound of a horse's hooves came from around the bend in the road. In this state there was no way she could speak coherently or make explanations about her odd clothes. She jumped behind the nearest rosebush. Taking her eyes off the place where the door had dematerialized made her feel even more as though the last link to the portal—to her whole world—was gone.

The horse and rider came into view, traveling at a leisurely pace. *Get on with it,* she thought. All she wanted to do was return to the spot where she'd been standing. What if—somehow—Jack was looking through the door at this very moment and couldn't see her? What would he think? What would he do?

Finally the traveler moved down the road and out of sight. She returned to what she hoped was the same place she'd been standing when this disaster started.

After what seemed like forever, she heard bells. At first she thought they were coming from the church nearby.

But then she realized it was the sound of magic in the air around her, tinkling and glittering.

The animator is working again!

A few more moments passed, and along with the ringing of the bells she heard Jack's voice, small and frantically calling from somewhere far off. "Ruthie! Where are you?"

The patio slowly reappeared around her; there were a few flickers, and then the hazy outline of a brick wall came into focus and gained substance, like a hologram solidifying. Then the door came rushing toward her, as though it might knock her down, stopping just inches away from her, with Jack standing right in the middle of it. He looked as terrified as she felt.

"Ruthie!" Jack yelled before the doorway was fully solid. He leapt out to the patio.

"What happened?" Ruthie managed to get out as her whole body unclenched.

"I'm sorry! I forgot that we hadn't figured out what the animator was yet. I picked up a vase from the mantel . . . I thought I could bring it outside. It turned out to be the animator," Jack tried to explain.

"But why?" Her rattled nerves still rumbled.

"I had the idea that maybe we could put the toad in something old out here," he explained, "since things that are the true antiques have the ability to go back and forth—like the ring dial," Jack explained. "I thought maybe they might have a little extra power; you could put the toad inside something and it might work like a time-defying container. And you'd get to keep the toad."

"That's pretty out there," Ruthie said, rubbing her hands along her arms to check her solidity.

"I realized what happened after I had the vase halfway across the room. But I had to run out to the corridor because people were coming. I'm really sorry!"

"What took so long for the door to reappear?"

"A tour group stopped in front of the viewing window, so I had to wait."

"No more messing with the animators, okay?"

"Right."

Her heart rate returning to normal, Ruthie looked at the carving in her hand. "It *would* be incredible to be able to keep this."

They stood there silently, mulling the possibilities.

"Your idea still might work. See if you can find another real antique—another vase or a box or something—and bring it out here."

Jack slipped back into the room. Ruthie didn't like this, being alone in the eighteenth century while Jack was in the twenty-first, knowing how easily the connection between the two worlds could be broken. So she set the toad down and stepped inside the room. Jack quickly found another vase, an ashy white one with an ebony lid—one of a pair resting on two tall pedestals.

"This seems old," he said, and then they both walked out onto the patio. The vase transformed before their eyes from a crackled, delicate-looking antique to a brand-new vase, its surface glossy and smooth, the grayed glaze returning to its original ivory. Ruthie placed the carving inside and Jack put the lid back on.

They crossed the threshold. As expected, the vase aged rapidly, looking as it had only moments before. Jack lifted the lid and peered into the dark interior. "It's still here!"

Ruthie inhaled. "I can't believe it!" The vase had carried the toad safely through almost three centuries!

"You know what this means?" Jack asked.

"It means we can bring stuff back from the past," Ruthie answered.

"Every time we come here, we learn something else that the magic can do," Jack observed.

"I know," Ruthie said. "But I'm not sure bringing things back from the past is a good idea. It doesn't seem like we should be able to."

"Almost feels like cheating."

"Exactly."

"But Freddy gave it to you. It's not stealing," Jack reminded her. "Maybe this is just a onetime thing . . . or maybe when we take it out . . ."

Jack tipped the vase and the toad—now darkened and cracked with age—tumbled out into Ruthie's palm.

But something else spilled out with it.

Next to the toad rested a letter written in elegant script on yellowed stationery.

Jack picked it up and read aloud:

February 20, 1939

To whom it may concern,
    I am compelled to write. I have reason to
believe that the key belonging to me is in your
possession. You may feel your work in the studio
gives you certain rights but this item was
purchased on my behalf, paid for with my funds.
I consider it to be one of my prize possessions.
    This is a most serious—dare I say dangerous—
matter, as the key must be returned to its proper
place in the looking-glass box. Do not try to
search for the box; I have taken it with me to
Santa Barbara, where it is secure in my vault.
Upon my return to Chicago, I hope this matter will
be put to rest.
                    I remain anxiously,
                    Narcissa Thorne
                    Montjoie, Santa Barbara, California

Ruthie took some moments to process what she'd just
heard. "I can't believe it!" she was finally able to say.

"Check the key—is it doing anything?"

Ruthie quickly looked inside her bag and saw flashes.
She lifted the key for Jack to see.

Ruthie exhaled loudly. "Now what?" This morning
all she had wanted to do was explore a few rooms and
secret worlds. Even though the letter was addressed to

"To whom it may concern," Ruthie felt like it was written to her and Jack. After all, they had possession of the key. And even though they hadn't been the ones who had stolen it, it was loot that needed to be returned. But how? And to whom?

"Almost there," Jack said in the dark air duct high above the ceiling of Gallery 11.

They were making their way to the American corridor and room A2, where the hourglass belonged. In this lightless tunnel Ruthie's nerves felt brittle, and the words from Mrs. Thorne's letter—*a most serious and dangerous matter*—repeated in her head. It was one thing to put the hourglass in its proper place. But how could they possibly return the key?

The American rooms were set in an island in the middle of Gallery 11, and this was the way Ruthie and Jack traveled there. A crochet chain that Ruthie had made for them to climb up and into the duct also worked like a mountain climber's rope to guide their way through the darkness. The dull glow coming from the back of the rooms finally appeared through the vent ahead of them.

"When you get down to the ledge, go to the right," Ruthie said, maneuvering out of the duct after Jack.

"Okay," Jack replied. To speed the descent, Jack was trying a new technique: instead of putting his feet in the loops of yarn, he placed them flat against the wall and grabbed hold of the loops with only his hands. His body was in a horizontal position, as if he were walking down the side of a skyscraper. "Try it, Ruthie," he called up to her.

It took more arm strength than their usual way, but it was also easier because she didn't have to find the loops to place her feet into. It was more like rappelling down a mountain, except she didn't push off too hard, making it something like a hop and a glide. "It's faster," Ruthie said, getting the hang of it. In no time they were on the ledge racing toward the New Hampshire room.

Scouting for the way in, they eased themselves through a tight space in the framework. It led into a side room with a narrow staircase made of rich, glowing wood. From this vantage point, they peered into the main room.

"What's this room?" Jack asked.

"Portsmouth, New Hampshire, around 1710. It's a copy of a room from the house of a man named John Wentworth, according to the catalogue."

"I think it's all clear," Jack whispered.

Softly they walked into the quiet space, trying to tell if the room was alive or not. The room was furnished simply, with everything made of wood, from the wide floorboards to an entirely paneled wall. The furniture too was wooden and had a heavier, blockier feel than the European rooms from the same era. A rustic chandelier hung over a table in the middle of the room, where they found some of the smallest items Mrs. Thorne ever created: a pair of eyeglasses, an open Bible that they could actually read, and a basket of knitting complete with ivory needles. Ruthie had seen them so many times from the gallery side that it was jarring to see them in front of her, just her size.

Ruthie checked the view out the window. Even though it was hard to tell from across the room, she thought the scene was only a painted diorama: bare trees covered with snow and a drab winter landscape beyond.

"Does it seem alive to you?"

"Not sure . . . I hear something but I don't know where it's coming from."

There was another door on the same side of the room from which they'd entered. Ruthie opened it and saw that it was a dark closet. Looking at a big cabinet next to it, Ruthie said, "This is where the hourglass belongs. On the top."

"How do you know?"

"The catalogue photo shows one right up there. I'm positive." Ruthie took the hourglass from her messenger bag. She had just put it in place when they heard voices from the gallery.

"Quick, in here!" Jack said. They fell into the closet and closed the door.

Jack got his phone out of his pocket and turned on the flashlight function, aiming it around the small space. Just as in other rooms with closets, they saw garments hanging from hooks. "Looks like we can go exploring!"

In the dim light, the clothes appeared to be very

similar in style to what they had worn when they met Jack Norfleet on Cape Cod in the 1730s, although these clothes were made of heavy woolen fabric. There were two dark cloaks, one knee-length, the other longer. They guessed the shorter one would be for a male, the long one for a female. This time there were shoes too, and they looked like the kind Pilgrims had worn at the first Thanksgiving.

"I think that door on the far side of the fireplace must be to the outside," Jack said.

"Let's put these on over our clothes. The view out the windows is a winter scene, so if it's alive it might be cold," Ruthie advised. When they had the buttons buttoned and the shoes buckled, they cracked the closet door.

"All clear," Jack said. He headed straight for the door. Ruthie followed.

The brass doorknob was stiff and took some effort to open, but he managed. The door creaked as he pulled it open.

"What is this?" Ruthie asked when she looked through the door.

Instead of a wintry landscape, they were looking into another stairwell, exactly like the one they had just been in, only now they were at the very top of the stairs. They proceeded down. A velvet rope barricade was stretched across the base so that no one could climb the stairs. They ducked under it. The stairwell opened to a furnished room that was almost identical to the one they just left.

Like A2, this room had a low, beamed ceiling, one wall

paneled in lustrous wood with a massive brick-lined fireplace, and a table in the middle of the room with carved wooden chairs. Some of the details were different, but the room was remarkably similar.

"Weird," Jack said. "This is déjà vu!"

"It feels like we're in another Thorne Room," Ruthie observed.

"But there are four walls—no big viewing window out to Gallery 11," Jack added.

"And why would Mrs. Thorne have built an almost identical room connected to the first?" Ruthie wondered. "It's like she did two versions—"

"Who's that?" Jack interrupted. Through the small glass panes of a window on the far wall he saw people go by—people of their size, not the large humans looking in from the museum. They didn't seem to be wearing eighteenth-century clothing.

But they weren't wearing twenty-first-century clothing either!

The women wore dresses that fitted tightly at their waists, and they carried small handbags. Their hair was mostly short and stiffly styled, and they wore dainty little hats. The men had on dark suits, some double-breasted, and they all wore ties.

And then a lady stopped and looked in—right at Ruthie and Jack. There was no time to hide, so they stood still.

"What's going on?" Ruthie asked.

"Could this be some sort of parallel world?" Jack mused.

"It looks so similar to the rooms—but who are those people?" Ruthie was thoroughly confused.

Then a man and woman walked in from a different door.

"Oh, this is new," the man said, smiling at them.

"Very charming," the woman said.

They admired the costumed Jack and Ruthie and then walked off the way they'd come.

"What's happening?" Jack whispered.

A family came into the room with a young boy and girl who coyly wanted to touch the fabric of Ruthie's cloak. She let them and smiled, not wanting to draw attention.

When they left Ruthie said, "Obviously, A2 is not a portal to the eighteenth century! That stairway leading up to the Thorne Rooms door we came through—it must be part of the portal area." Ruthie nodded toward it. "I don't think anyone else can see it. No one's going up. People aren't even looking in."

"Let's get out of these clothes and find out what's going on," Jack said.

While the room was empty they quickly shed the heavy outer garments and shoes, tossing them in a big cabinet— just in time, as more people wandered through. In their own clothes and shoes, Ruthie and Jack weren't dressed quite like these people, but at least they didn't look like they were from the eighteenth century anymore.

"Let's see what's out there." Ruthie pointed to the door that the other people had used.

When they looked through the door they found they were looking into yet another room.

Neither of them recognized this as one of the Thorne Rooms, but it too could pass for one if made small. They walked in. The bare floor consisted of wide boards, and all the furniture was also made of dark carved wood. Another huge brick-lined fireplace took up most of an entire wall. An imposing bed filled one corner of the space, its canopy and curtains made of a rich red fabric. Through windows with diagonal leaded panes they saw a steady stream of people passing by.

"Look," Ruthie said, running over to a sign on the wall. "It says this is the Thomas Hart House in Ipswich, Massachusetts, from 1680."

Suddenly a surly man in a uniform charged into the room. "Have you seen any reenactors in here?" he growled.

Ruthie's eyes fell on the man's ID pin. Printed below his name she saw *The Metropolitan Museum of Art.*

"There were two people in costume in that room," Jack answered truthfully.

"I don't know who people think they are these days . . . ," the man said, storming off.

"Did you see his ID?" Ruthie said under her breath. "We're in the Metropolitan Museum of Art in New York City!"

"How did we end up here? A2 was supposed to be New Hampshire."

"I have no idea, but we'd better find out. Come on!" Ruthie said, and headed out of the room.

They walked down the hallway with the windows through which they'd seen people walking by. At least that made sense now.

A map on the wall proved it: they were in the historic reproduction rooms in the Metropolitan Museum, one of the largest art museums in the world.

"This is so cool—I've always wanted to come here," Ruthie exclaimed. "My favorite book is set in the Met."

"Which one?"

From the Mixed-Up Files of Mrs. Basil E. Frankweiler."

"Oh, right. That's a good one," Jack agreed.

They studied another map along the way and found a route through the maze-like spaces to the lobby. First they passed through more period rooms (Ruthie wondering which room Claudia from *The Mixed-Up Files* might have slept in), and they had to remind themselves that they weren't in miniature rooms any longer. Then gallery after gallery of paintings and sculptures, and people—New Yorkers!—ambling through. They saw Rembrandts and huge paintings that took up entire walls. Statues of men and women from Greek and Roman times gazed blankly into space with their white marble eyes.

Finally they reached the grand front lobby, which was

at least triple the size of the Art Institute's. The arched ceiling soared high overhead, and the doors to the city stood in front of them, just past a row of tall fluted columns.

"Ready to explore?"

Thinking about the letter from Mrs. Thorne, Ruthie took a half second longer to answer than she might have otherwise. But the most exciting city in the world was just paces away. "Are you kidding?" Ruthie answered. "I've never been to New York City!"

· · · 5 · · ·

NEW YORK, NEW YORK

"SO THIS IS NEW YORK!" Ruthie exclaimed as they stood just outside the doors to the Metropolitan Museum of Art, looking down on Fifth Avenue.

The avenue was filled with people. So were the museum steps. Some seemed to be tourists, looking at maps, and even though it was a warm summer day almost everyone—certainly most of the men—wore hats.

Across the street buildings rose high, maybe twenty stories or so. To the immediate right they saw the south wing of the museum and the stone wall that surrounded New York's Central Park. Beyond that, they saw the tops of a few skyscrapers, including the distinctive spire of the Empire State Building.

The cars that drove by were black—except for the taxicabs, which were multicolored, mostly yellow and white, green and white, or red and white, with black and white checkerboard strips along the sides.

"Look at the cars! I feel like I'm in an old gangster movie," Jack said.

Ruthie pointed across the avenue. "There's a newsstand over there. Let's get a paper and find out what year it is."

They got a few funny looks from people. Ruthie was suddenly conscious of the fact that no one was wearing sneakers like she and Jack were—and that she seemed to be the only girl in sight wearing pants. They passed by a couple of apartment buildings with uniformed doormen posted under long awnings.

"Excuse me," Jack said to one of the doormen, "what time do you have?"

"Coming up on two o'clock," he replied after pulling a pocket watch from his breast pocket.

A few paces on, Jack took his own watch from his pocket, and Ruthie inquired, "Why did you ask him?"

"I'm still trying to figure out how time works outside the rooms. My watch says it's five minutes after twelve."

"Remember what we figured—that the time is set by the diorama scene. Anyway, I'm glad you have a watch, so we won't lose track of what time it is in our world."

Just down the street they arrived at the newsstand, which sold newspapers, maps and souvenirs for tourists, and a few magazines and comic books. Color splashed the covers of titles like *Action Comics, Marvel Mystery Comics,*

and *All American Comics*. Superheroes heaved cars above their heads, while muscle-bound good guys socked villains off their feet. *Bam* and *wham* blared across the pictures in bold lettering.

They checked out the pile of newspapers: the *Herald,* the *New York Tribune,* the *Daily News.* They chose a copy of the *New York Times.*

"Three cents!" Jack exclaimed when he saw the price printed just under the bold Gothic letters.

"You're telling me, kid," the man behind the counter said. "The price of everything's going through the roof these days!"

Jack fished three pennies from his pocket and was about to pay when he suddenly stopped, turning his back to the man. He held the coins in his palm for Ruthie to see.

"What is it?" she asked.

"They feel warm."

And then they both saw it—the slightest little glimmer around the spot where the date on the penny was. Ruthie kept her eye on one of the pennies and saw it transform from a brown 1992 penny into a shiny new 1939 coin. Her mouth fell open.

"I guess this makes sense," Ruthie said under her breath. "We can't leave things here that don't exist yet. I bet that's what year we're in."

"That's awesome!"

Jack turned back around and handed the man the now shiny pennies.

"'June twenty-second,'" Ruthie read from the masthead.

"That answers that question. But I can't get over that it only cost three cents!" Jack said. Then he added, "I just thought of something."

"I know," Ruthie put in, reading his mind. "*Everything* is going to be a lot cheaper now." The possibilities of what could be purchased with the modest amount of money in her pocket danced in her mind.

"Do you see the comic books at the back of the stand?" Jack asked.

"What about them?"

"The one that's called *Detective Comics*—it's got Batman on the cover. It's the first one! I'm sure of it. Nineteen thirty-nine. And they're only ten cents each! Now that we know how to get stuff across the portal, I could bring one home. It'd be worth hundreds of dollars!"

Ruthie bit her lip. Something didn't feel quite right, but she couldn't put her finger on it. After all, she'd gotten to keep the toad from Freddy. Why shouldn't Jack get a copy of a first-edition comic book? She couldn't think of a reason. "True. You could even buy a few copies."

"You're right." He took a quarter and a nickel from his pocket and watched the faces of Washington and Jefferson lose their scuff marks and the dates change in his cupped hand. He plunked them on the counter. "Three *Detective Comics* books, please."

"Here you go, lad. These things are selling like hotcakes."

They crossed Fifth Avenue again and found an empty bench just inside an entrance to Central Park.

Jack glanced at the cover of the Batman comic book, which read, *Starting This Issue: The Amazing and Unique Adventures of Batman!* "I'll read this later. Let's see what's in the paper."

Looking over the front page, they saw lots of articles about how the Nazis were threatening other countries. It looked like China and Japan were at war. Jack filled Ruthie in on what he knew about this time in history.

"World War Two started when Germany invaded Poland—September first, I think," Jack told her. "But the United States didn't get in till after Pearl Harbor."

A rough-looking man came by walking a dog. He sat down next to them. "Nice weather. You two from out of town?" the man asked.

"Chicago," Jack answered. "How could you tell?"

"Your clothes," he said, his eyes landing on their shoes. "Where'd you get those?"

"They're the newest thing at home," Ruthie replied.

"You here for the World's Fair?"

Ruthie and Jack looked at each other, thinking the same thing: *Another World's Fair?* Not long ago they had visited the 1937 Fair in Paris, outside of room E27.

"Uh, sure," Jack began.

" 'The World of Tomorrow.' They got everything there, even a talking robot," he said. "But who needs a talking robot? Specially if we all kill each other in the war they say's coming."

"We were just looking in the paper to see if there's anything about the fair," Ruthie explained.

"Seems like all the news these days is bad news," the man commented. "Even the sports pages." He shook his head.

"What do you mean?" Jack asked, flipping through the paper.

"Didn't you hear? The Iron Horse . . . ," the man started to say, but he choked up and couldn't finish his sentence.

On the first page of the sports section, Ruthie and Jack saw the headline:

INFANTILE PARALYSIS TERMINATES GEHRIG'S PLAYING CAREER, FORCED TO QUIT BASEBALL

"Oh, man," Jack said.

The dog tugged on the leash, and the man rose. "So sad. Bye now."

"Sad is right," Jack sighed, returning to looking at the paper.

"Looks like a lot happened in 1939," Ruthie observed. "Anyway, what do you want to do?"

"Whatever we can do in a few hours—my mom wants us home by five o'clock."

"Okay."

"How much money do you have?" Jack asked.

"About fifteen dollars. How about you?"

"Thirty bucks."

"You know, since everything is so cheap now, we could do lots," Ruthie pointed out. "I say we take a cab to the fair. I'm sure we can afford one."

They headed back to the sidewalk facing Fifth Avenue and stood at the curb with their arms raised to wave down a taxicab. Several zoomed by, but in a few minutes they were climbing into the back of a yellow and white New York City cab.

"These are roomy!" Jack said. "No seats belts, though."

"You kids got money?" the cabbie asked.

"Yes," they answered in unison.

"Where to?"

"The World's Fair, please," Ruthie answered.

Ruthie gazed out the windows. Everything looked different: the clothes, the signs, the cars, even the street lamps. As the taxi stopped for a red light, Ruthie saw a food vendor at the corner with his cart. The cart had large wheels with wooden spokes, like the kind on covered wagons, and a big black umbrella on top. The sign on the cart read: Frankfurters, Sauerkraut and Onions, Soft Drinks, All Kinds of Pies, All Five Cents Each.

"I recognize some of the buildings from when my mom took me here a couple of years ago at Christmas. Actually, it was many years from *now*! Everything sure looks newer!" Jack observed.

They traveled all the way from Eightieth Street to the southern border of Central Park at Fifty-Ninth Street before the cab turned left. After a few blocks they reached the ramp to the Queensboro Bridge. The complicated metal span loomed in front of the cab, breaking the sunlight into little bits.

"It reminds me of the Eiffel Tower, the way the metal looks like lace," Ruthie said.

"It took eight years to build," Jack added.

"How do you know that?"

"*Charlotte's Web.* Charlotte tells Wilbur that."

Through the beams and girders of the bridge, a view of the busy river appeared down below. It was filled with boats of all shapes and sizes, including tugboats spewing thick smoke.

The bridge delivered them to the other side of the East River and they passed through a neighborhood with a very different look from Manhattan. The buildings were smaller and less grand, and trees lined many of the streets. Soon big banner-like signs for the fair appeared, with images of two pure white structures, a large sphere and a tall pointed spike-like tower.

"Those are called the Trylon and Perisphere," the cabbie said. "They built the longest escalator in the world inside. Don't miss it!" The cabbie pulled over and stopped at the curb in front of the entrance. "That'll be a dollar forty."

Jack counted out the amount—a dollar and four

dimes—watching the tiny flares as the face of FDR changed to the god Mercury on the ten-cent coins. He placed the money in the driver's open hand and added another dime for a tip.

Ruthie and Jack hopped out and found themselves at the main entrance to the fair, a steady stream of people filing in. Everyone looked dressed up—just like at the Metropolitan Museum.

"Look," Jack said, pointing to the sign at the admission booth, "only twenty-five cents for kids!" The cashier handed them a guide booklet with their tickets.

As soon as they passed through the entry gate the white spire and globe that they'd seen on the signs came into view over the tops of the other structures. Five-car trams and slow-moving tour buses shared the path with thousands of pedestrians. One pavilion was devoted to railroads and another to aviation. Ruthie read the names of American car companies boldly posted over the entrances of the first buildings they passed: Ford, Chrysler. The huge General Motors pavilion had a long line of people snaking out to the main path.

Jack checked the guide. "Futurama—the World of 1960! Ha!"

Most of the buildings looked sleek and modern. Dozens of colorful flags blew in the gentle breeze. The fair was so large and there was so much to look at that several times Ruthie and Jack bumped into people who were also not watching where they were going.

They arrived at the two huge white structures. Jack read, "'The spire is taller than the Washington Monument and the Perisphere is a hundred and eighty-five feet in diameter.'" The giant sphere sat in the middle of a moat, sunlight glinting from the water and reflecting off the stark white surface. A long ramp—the guidebook said it was called the Helicline—wrapped around the sphere from the middle down to the ground. Fair visitors disappeared into a small door at the base of the spire. The line for this wasn't long, so they went in.

"Didn't the cab driver tell us this was the biggest escalator in the world?" Ruthie asked once they were inside and looking up at the moving stair.

"That's right," a man in front of them said. "A real feat of engineering, it is!" He gave a whistle.

It *was* tall, Ruthie thought, but she'd seen some just as big. "What's at the top?"

"An exhibit called Democracity," the man answered. "I'm going for my second time. It shows how the world is going to look in the year 2039."

The escalator whisked them up inside the Perisphere.

"Wow," Jack said. Ruthie nodded.

At about the widest point around the perimeter ran two balconies, one on top of the other. It was as though you were in an enormous dome-shaped movie theater looking at the main floor from the balcony seats, only spread out below was what the man had referred to: a giant diorama called Democracity. The balconies slowly rotated to allow a good look at the whole scene.

"It's like a huge setup for model trains," Jack said.

The diorama consisted of countryside, small towns, and a big, glistening city in the center. There were roads and rivers, hills and forests—all to scale and laid out neatly.

From loudspeakers hidden throughout the sphere they heard a man's somber voice: *"The city of man and the world of tomorrow. Here are grass and trees and stone and steal. Not a dream city but a symbol of life as lived by the man of tomorrow . . ."*

The audience listened in silence while the balconies steadily revolved.

"The good life of the well-planned city . . . Here, brain and brawn, faith and courage are linked in high endeavor as men march on toward unity and peace."

"Sheesh! Only men?" Ruthie whispered, perturbed.

"Yeah. Unity and peace? I guess whoever dreamed this up didn't figure on World War Two coming." Jack pointed to the teardrop-shaped vehicles on the lightly trafficked city streets. "I'd drive one of those."

"I wonder . . . We're in 1939. This miniature was made at about the same time Mrs. Thorne was working on hers. Do you think she's seen . . . she *saw* this one?"

"She probably knew about it, at least." Jack looked at his watch. "We should go if we want to see anything else."

They wended their way around the balcony to the exit and back out into the sunshine. At the bottom of the winding ramp a vendor sold souvenir buttons. One read *I Have Seen the Future.*

"If he only knew . . . ," Ruthie said under her breath.

Jack checked the map. "Elektro the Robot. How about it?"

"Sure."

They walked down a promenade called the Court of Power and turned right at the Plaza of Light.

The building they arrived at looked as though it had been made for an old science fiction movie. In front of it stood a tower consisting of a tall center pole surrounded by five rings. A sign explained that a time capsule was buried under the base, to be opened in five thousand years.

"Five thousand years?" Ruthie asked, astonished.

"That'd be like us finding something from before the time of the pyramids," Jack calculated.

"See Elektro, the amazing thinking robot!" an announcement blared out of a loudspeaker. "Starting now!"

"Perfect timing," Ruthie said, and they scooted in to get a good view.

The room was buzzing with excitement. A boy near them said to his sister, "They say he can walk backward too!"

Everything inside was glass and metal and shiny—the ultimate in modern style for 1939, but Ruthie couldn't help but think how old-fashioned it all looked. Her impression was confirmed when she and Jack looked up. On a balcony in front of them a man in a suit and tie spoke with dramatic flourish into a microphone.

"It returns! The thing with almost a human brain: Elektro the Robot!"

A door behind the man opened and out came a tall, silvery metal man-like robot. It glided smoothly but very slowly to the center of the balcony, staring straight ahead, its legs hardly moving. To Ruthie it looked an awful lot like the Tin Woodsman from the *Wizard of Oz*, minus the pointy hat. People down below gazed up, oohing and aah ing. Then it spoke.

"I. Am. Elektro. Mightiest. Of. All. Robots. I. Am. Seven. Feet. Six. Inches. Tall. My. Brain. Is. Bigger. Than. Yours. It. Weighs. Sixty. Pounds."

Then another man—this one in a lab coat—appeared and put a balloon in Elektro's mouth, saying, "Elektro, I command you to blow up the balloon and break it."

The balloon expanded and burst, and the audience erupted in applause and cheering.

"You've gotta be kidding me!" Jack said in a low voice. "That's it?"

"Not even as good as the early Star Wars movies."

Jack checked his watch. "We should go anyway."

The walkways outside were even more crowded now. A large family took up most of the space in front of them— the mom was pushing a stroller, the dad was carrying a toddler, and there were another five kids holding hands and walking. The youngest of those was crying about something. Suddenly, while Ruthie watched, he yanked free from his older sister's hand and darted away—straight into the path of an oncoming tram!

"Jack—look!" Ruthie screamed.

Jack had seen it too and before she finished the words he had dashed in front of the child, scooped him up in his arms, and carried him out of the way, tumbling to the ground with him. The tram screeched to a halt. Stunned, the boy, who looked to be about four years old, temporarily quieted.

"Billy!" the mother cried out, and ran to them.

The tram driver turned off the motor and stepped off, shaking. "Are you all right? The little guy came out of nowhere and I couldn't stop fast enough. I could've killed him. Thank you, son!" He reached down to help Jack up.

The mother hugged her child tightly and then Jack. The commotion grew, with more and more people gathering.

Ruthie made her way into the cluster in time to hear the father say, "This boy saved my son's life!"

Jack looked at Ruthie, somewhat dumbstruck. A few people with cameras came up, some wanting to know Jack's name. A police officer arrived. Ruthie started to feel uneasy, especially when she heard someone say, "He should be on the front page of the paper!"

"Where are your parents?" the father asked. "I'd like to tell them what a swell son they have!"

"That's right!" the mother said, hugging Jack again.

Jack reluctantly gave his name before Ruthie jumped in, saying, "We have to go. Our parents are waiting for us. Sorry!" She grabbed Jack by the hand and tore him away. People called after them, but Ruthie and Jack didn't turn around. They ran all the way back to the fair entrance and didn't stop until they saw the taxi stand. They were panting hard.

"You saved that kid's life," Ruthie finally said.

"I guess I did. Pretty wild, huh?"

"Just think. If we hadn't by chance ended up in New York . . ." The consequences of what had happened were coming into sharper focus—along with the words *a most serious and dangerous matter* from Mrs. Thorne's letter. "There was nothing we did that made that little kid run into the path of the tram. That was going to happen whether we were there or not. But you stopped it from happening! You changed his history."

"I know. By chance."

···6···
THE WOODEN BOX

BY THE TIME THEY ARRIVED back at the museum, they had to rush in order to be at Jack's house by five o'clock. The Art Institute no longer felt like a maze to them, but here in the Metropolitan, they had to ask directions to the room from the Thomas Hart House twice.

While Jack worried about the time, Ruthie worried silently about the portal. Arriving in New York City in 1939 when they thought they'd be in eighteenth-century New Hampshire introduced a pesky uncertainty to her understanding of how the time travel worked. Winding through the museum, she thought, *What if the portal is invisible now and we're stuck in New York the way I was stuck in England?* Could this be what Mrs. Thorne's warning referred to? And then she heard Mrs. McVittie's voice in her head, saying, *Question assumptions.*

"Here we are," Jack said as they turned the corner and saw the impressive red canopy bed. "Through there."

They backtracked to the Thomas Hart room and then the Wentworth room and the stairwell that led up to the door to A2, which would—*hopefully*, Ruthie thought—bring them back to Mrs. Thorne's version of the room. The velvet rope still hung across the staircase. They slipped under it and darted up the stairs. Ruthie exhaled when she saw the door.

She turned the heavy knob and cracked the door. But then she remembered something. "The clothes—we left them in the cabinet downstairs."

"Here, hold these. I'll go get them." Jack handed her his comics.

Ruthie didn't like having him out of her sight while she waited in the dark stairwell. She tried to think what she could use from the room to carry the comics through the portal and across time.

"Is it all clear?" Jack asked when he reappeared with the clothes in his arms.

Ruthie opened the door an inch. She didn't see anyone but put her finger to her lips and listened. "I think so. I'll see what I can find to put the comics in."

Ruthie stacked the comics on top of the clothes and slipped back into room A2. Taking a quick inventory, she decided there just weren't many items in this sparsely decorated room that might work. The only book was a Bible, but it was prominently placed right in the center of the room and was something museum visitors always marveled over. Taking it out even temporarily seemed risky. And most likely it had been made by one of Mrs. Thorne's craftsmen, so it wouldn't work, because the item needed to be a real antique. Or did it? Since this room had been created at the same time as the era it was a portal to, would that make it old enough? The complexity of this time twist tangled up like a knot in her head.

Then she noticed a box. It was about as big as an oversized jewelry box, made of dark stained wood. She picked it up and headed back toward the stairwell where Jack was waiting. But she paused for a second. What if this was the animator? She didn't want to make the same mistake that Jack had made.

"Jack?" she said in a loud whisper at the door.

"What?"

Whew! It's not the animator. Ruthie opened the door.

"We can try this," she said as she met him on the other side. No sooner had she spoken than the color of the wood softened. It was a subtle change but noticeable. "It just got about seventy-five years younger."

"But it still looks old," Jack said.

The light was dim in the stairwell. Lifting the hinged top, Jack's sharp eyes spied something on the bottom. He reached in and pulled out not one item but two.

In his open palm Jack held two rings, completely different in style. One was ornate, made of what looked like real, shining gold. They saw an enameled image of a lion and a unicorn on either side of a crowned sphere surrounded by vines, all encircled with tiny rubies and emeralds. The other was a cheap mood ring, the kind that can be found in dollar stores and junk shops.

"What are these doing in here?" Jack asked.

"There's no way either of these were made by Mrs. Thorne; I'm pretty sure she didn't make any jewelry for the rooms. Rings are way too small!" Ruthie inspected the gold ring, trying to see any markings on the inside of the band. "I think it's old."

"But this one can't be very old," Jack said, still holding the mood ring. "Do you think Dr. Bell might've left them in here?"

"She'll be at your house; we can ask her before dinner," Ruthie replied. "Let's put everything in the box and go."

They placed the two rings and the three comics in the box, closed the lid, and waited until they heard no voices from Gallery 11; then they stepped into the room. Jack returned the clothes to the closet while Ruthie set the box back where it belonged. She waited for Jack before opening it.

Jack grinned as soon as they lifted the lid. "Ha! It worked again!" The three comic books looked much older than they had moments ago but were still in excellent condition, as if they'd been sitting in that box aging undisturbed for three-quarters of a century.

Ruthie took out the two rings, which looked almost

unchanged. She opened her messenger bag and saw Freddy's toad just as she had left it. She added the rings and Jack carefully slid in the comics. "Let's go," she said, and Jack followed, still smiling.

Out on the ledge Jack looked at his watch. "It's after four o'clock. We'd better move fast."

They stayed small and made their way back to the European Corridor. Once there, to save time, Ruthie tossed the key and leapt to the ground, expanding in midair. If there was one thing about the magic that she wished she could carry into her regular life, it was this; in those few seconds of weightlessness, she felt as free as a bird gliding to the ground.

Jack sat, still small, on the ledge, dangling his feet like he didn't have a care in the world. Ruthie retrieved the crochet chain and then lifted her tiny friend to the floor. Then she shrank once again so they could scoot under the access door together.

As they came up the stairs to the main floor of the museum—full size—Ruthie thought about how happy she was that they were going to see the Bells. She hadn't seen either one of them for a while. Meeting Edmund Bell when he still worked as a guard in the museum was possibly the most important meeting she'd ever had. He was the person who had let Jack sneak a peek in the dark corridor behind the rooms, where Jack caught the first glimpse of the magic key. When it turned out his daughter, Dr. Caroline Bell, had magically visited the rooms as a little girl (which Ruthie and Jack were pretty sure Mr. Bell didn't know about), they'd found a helpful ally when they needed to protect the rooms from a thief.

Approaching the big glass doors that opened onto Michigan Avenue, Ruthie said, "I hope we'll have a chance to show Dr. Bell—" She stopped in midsentence and grabbed her messenger bag.

"What?" Jack asked when he saw the look on her face.

"I think it just got lighter," she responded, not wanting to open the canvas bag and verify what she was afraid had just happened. But she looked in anyway.

Crestfallen, she held it out for Jack. His shoulders slumped.

The comic books were gone, as was Freddy's carved toad. At the doors to the museum, the magic had ceased working and the past had reclaimed the four treasures.

"I guess it was too good to be true," Ruthie admitted. "We can't bring the stuff from the past to our time."

"It's kind of like what happened when we tried to take my shrunken bento box out of the museum still small, remember? We already knew the magic doesn't hold far from the rooms. We should have figured."

"I know, but I thought this would be different." Ruthie sighed deeply. "Because Freddy *gave* me the toad. And you *bought* the comics. Because we were able to get them across the portals."

"But my knife—the one from Jack Norfleet? Why do I still have that?" Jack wondered, thinking about the whale-tooth knife made by his pirate ancestor.

"Because Jack Norfleet put it in his desk centuries ago. And remember, Mrs. Thorne got that desk as an antique and magically shrank it. The knife is a true antique—it was already in the desk when Mrs. Thorne got it. We didn't try to make it skip over all those years. That's what the magic won't let us do."

"Right. It gets so confusing. I should add all that to the list of rules I made a while back," Jack said. "The rings—they must still be in your bag. The mood ring can't even be as old as the Thorne Rooms."

"And the letter!" Ruthie said, plunging her hand to the bottom of her bag. "Here it is," she exhaled.

She fished around in the bag again, her fingers finding the mood ring first. The antique ring seemed so old and otherworldly, Ruthie was half expecting it to have vanished. But she pulled it from her bag looking exactly as it had when she put it in. "This proves someone from our time put both rings in that box."

"How?"

"If someone had gone into the past and brought this old ring back—like we did with the comics and the toad—it would have disappeared. It has to be a true antique that someone left in that box."

They trudged through the doors and down the steps to the bus stop. The heat of the day was at its worst, rays of hot sunlight smacking them hard from the west. On the bus, all the riders, crammed shoulder to shoulder, made the sweltering air even warmer. They got off a few blocks early and walked to Jack's loft.

"You know," Ruthie began while Jack unlocked the building's door, "I wasn't really sure it was a good idea to bring things back from the past."

"Why not?"

"I can't really explain it. But somehow it seemed like we were sneaking around the rules of the magic."

Jack shrugged as they got on the elevator. "So you don't think rules are made to be broken?"

"All I know is that when I got stuck in the eighteenth century this morning, I didn't like it. We shouldn't assume that everything will turn out okay if we don't respect the magic."

"You're probably right. Especially since we have no idea how we ended up in 1939 New York today!"

Ruthie felt her taut nerves turn like a rubber band of a toy plane. "You don't think," she began, an idea forming as she spoke, "that we were—I don't know—*meant* to go back to the World's Fair? You know, so you could save Billy?"

Jack looked at her. "Anything's possible." He slid the elevator gate to the side and opened the door. "Hello!" Jack hollered into the spacious loft.

"We're back here," his mom called from her studio.

Ruthie and Jack headed to the studio, where Edmund and Caroline Bell were viewing Lydia's latest paintings.

"Isn't this nice to see you both!" Edmund Bell greeted them.

"Did you two have a good day? Did you stay cool out there?" Lydia asked.

"We spent most of it in the Art Institute," Jack answered.

"Really?" Dr. Bell said with a knowing look and a smile. "Anything special going on there?"

"The usual," Ruthie replied, smiling too and waiting for the right moment to tell her about what had happened today.

While Mr. Bell and Lydia talked about their work, Ruthie, Jack, and Dr. Bell drifted out of the studio and into Jack's house within the house, where they wouldn't be overheard. First they showed her the letter and asked her if she had ever come across anything like it in the rooms when she was a girl.

Dr. Bell read the letter. "This is remarkable. No, I never saw anything like this."

Then they told her about their time travel surprise.

"We can't explain it; we entered in the New Hampshire room from the 1700s, but we ended up in New York City in 1939," Ruthie said.

"Yeah," Jack added, "we were smack in the middle of the Metropolitan Museum of Art."

"Do you have a catalogue of the rooms, Jack? Maybe there's a clue," Dr. Bell suggested.

"Yep," he said, going to a stack of books on his bookshelf. "Right here."

Jack handed the catalogue to Ruthie. She opened to the page for A2 and she and Dr. Bell scanned the text. Dr. Bell pointed to a few lines. "I think that's your answer."

"What?" Jack asked.

"It says here that the Wentworth room came from a real house in New Hampshire," Dr. Bell said. "It was dismantled and reinstalled in the Metropolitan Museum of Art in New York. Mrs. Thorne copied that room in miniature. It doesn't say when. Why don't you check the Met's website?"

Jack went to his computer and found the site, typing "Wentworth room" in the search bar. Immediately an image of the room appeared. "There it is. Just like we saw."

"See that?" Dr. Bell pointed at the screen. " 'Sage Fund, 1926.' That tells you the name of the donor who paid for the room, and the year the museum acquired it."

In a few more clicks Jack had found an article about the opening of the new American period rooms at the Met. "It says they opened in December 1937."

"I get it!" Ruthie said. "Mrs. Thorne must have known about that and decided to make a miniature version. And since she made the American rooms in the late 1930s—"

"How do you know that?" Jack interrupted.

"I read it in the catalogue. That's why we ended up in that time."

"So it was a real, full-size eighteenth-century room but had been moved from New Hampshire to the Metropolitan Museum of Art," Jack said, sorting it out.

"Exactly. But because Mrs. Thorne was copying the museum room, it became a portal to New York City instead of New Hampshire."

"You must have been so surprised!" Dr. Bell added.

"I almost forgot." Ruthie grabbed her messenger bag and took out the two rings. "We were also surprised by these. We found them in a box in Mrs. Thorne's Wentworth room. I was wondering if you ever saw them when you were in the rooms, or if you put them there."

Dr. Bell studied them. "It was a long time ago, but no, these aren't familiar."

"If you didn't," Ruthie said, "who did?"

"Maybe whoever took the key in the first place," Jack suggested.

Dr. Bell held up the gem-encrusted one. In the light of Jack's room they saw wear and scratches on the gold that they hadn't been able to see before, making it look even older. "This one looks valuable. I think that's a family crest," she said, pointing to the carved lion and unicorn in the center of the ring.

"Jack, remember when you did that report last fall about medieval knights? Wasn't there something about family crests?"

"Yeah, they were symbols that represented family names. They put them on their shields and flags and stuff."

"And rings like this one," Dr. Bell explained. "I bet Minerva McVittie could help you identify it."

"She can also help with the hallmarks on the inside of

the band," Ruthie added, pointing to three stamped symbols: a leopard's head, the number 750, and the initials A.B. written in fancy script.

Dr. Bell looked at the other ring. "And this one looks like the mood rings that were popular when I was a kid. Do either of these have any magic?"

"Not that we've seen," Jack answered. "But that gives me an idea." He unsnapped the pocket of his cargo pants and pulled out Duchess Christina's key. "Put the mood ring next to it."

Ruthie set them side by side. Nothing happened.

"Try the other one," he suggested.

Ruthie switched the rings, and they all saw it at once: Christina's key beamed and glistened, like it had suddenly awakened, each magical flash setting off question after question in Ruthie's mind. But she was certain of one thing: it was trying to tell them something!

··· 7 ···
ONE CLUE CLOSER

IT WAS A SCORCHER AGAIN on Friday and Ruthie was happy to be back in the air-conditioned shop. When she was in the long dim space, with its walls lined with books, she felt as though she were deep in the recesses of a cool cave.

"If getting stuck in another century isn't enough warning, Narcissa Thorne's letter should be!" Mrs. McVittie declared after Ruthie and Jack recounted what had happened yesterday and showed her the letter. "She was clearly worried about the power of the key. This danger is all too real." Like Caroline Bell, Mrs. McVittie had also visited the rooms as a young girl, long ago. Although neither one of these grown-ups had experienced the time travel, they understood how it was possible, having held the magic key in their own hands.

"We're going to be more careful," Ruthie promised.

Mrs. McVittie looked skeptical. "And we're trying to figure a way to return the key."

Jack nudged Ruthie. "Show her the rings."

She set the bejeweled ring under the bright desk lamp. Jack placed the key right next to it and they watched it pulse steadily with light.

Mrs. McVittie eyed it through a magnifying glass that she kept at hand, ready for inspecting items such as this. "Interesting." She swiveled in her chair toward the shelf next to her and searched for a particular volume, which she opened in her lap.

"What's that?" Jack asked.

"A directory of family crests and coats of arms. It's a useful reference." She thumbed through the index. "We know the ring was made in England."

"How do you know?" Ruthie asked. "I didn't see the lion stamp."

"It's this leopard's head. That shows it came from London. Although sometimes with very old pieces, the markings aren't reliable." She held it for Ruthie to see, pointing with the tip of a pencil. "And the number 750 refers to the gold content. This is eighteen-karat."

"What about the initials, A.B.?" Jack wanted to know.

"Those could be the maker's initials, but I don't think they are because of the script. They look engraved, not stamped. I think they more likely belong to the owner of the ring."

That sounded enticing to Ruthie: one clue closer to . . . *what?*

"Here." Mrs. McVittie held up the book after a minute or two of searching. The page contained several coats of arms. They were all roughly shield-shaped, with lions, fleurs-de-lis, eagles, stags, and other symbols. "I think this may be a match."

They held the ring next to the image. It was nearly identical.

"It's the crest of the Brownlow family," Ruthie read. "Who were they?"

"You'll have to do some research on that," Mrs. McVittie answered. "But I suspect the initials belong to a member of that family."

"Can you tell how old it is?" Ruthie asked.

"Very old. I would place it in the early eighteenth century, perhaps even earlier," she answered. "You can tell by the cut of the gemstones."

While Ruthie and Mrs. McVittie spoke, Jack used his phone to search the name. "I found a few links," he said. "Have you ever heard of Belton House? It's some kind of mansion in England that you can take tours of. It's owned by a family named Brownlow. Look—here's the website."

Ruthie's eyes got wide as Jack held his phone for her to see. "Belton House! I know that name! Do you have the catalogue here, Mrs. McVittie?"

"Of course. Just over there." She pointed to the end of her reference shelves.

Ruthie leapt for it and swiped the pages open to one of the first rooms. "E4! I knew it!"

"Is that one we've been in?" Jack asked.

"Not yet. But listen to this: 'William Winde designed Belton House for the Bronlow family,'" she read. "It's spelled differently, '*Bron*low' instead of '*Brown*low,' but it must be the same! And it says, 'Mrs. Thorne was particularly drawn to this room.'"

"We seem to be getting somewhere!" Mrs. McVittie clapped her hands together.

"What else does it say?" Jack asked.

Ruthie scoured the page. "Not much else that's useful. Just stuff about the design of the room." She snapped the book shut. "We should take that ring into the room and investigate."

The L-shaped corridor that ran behind room E4 was short—sort of an extension of the main corridor after it was interrupted by the alcove. It was odd to be in this space, all in all only about ten feet long, compared with the main corridor, which ran behind the majority of the European rooms.

At the end was the huge thirteenth-century church room, by far the oldest period represented. Then came E1, Christina's room, where they had learned about the enchantment of the key and where Ruthie had magically heard the voice of Duchess Christina reading from her book. Next were two more English rooms and then E4, which was described as a drawing room.

After they had used the key to shrink and crawl under the access door, they got big again. Jack took the rolled-up ladder out of one of the pockets in his cargo pants. It worked perfectly when all they needed to do was climb to the ledge. He set it up and gave it a little tug to make sure it was secure.

"Before we get small we should try something," he began. "Maybe the ring's got the power to shrink you. Like my pirate coin. You were already small when you held it in the rooms, and then you put it in your bag."

"Good idea."

Jack took the ring from another pocket and dropped the jewel in her hand.

"You feel anything?"

Ruthie waited a few beats, then shook her head. She gave it back to Jack.

"I would've bet money it was going to shrink you!" he said, reaching down to pick up Christina's key from where it lay on the floor. He held the two together in his palm and once again the key flashed brightly in the dim light.

"There's no doubt—it's telling us something," Ruthie said. "But what?"

Jack handed the ring to her. "You might as well keep it now."

Ruthie dropped it in her messenger bag and then clasped Jack's hand, with Christina's key in the middle. The gentle gust swept around them and the space loomed huge once again.

By now they were expert climbers, and in no time they were on the ledge looking through the cracks in the framework to find the entrance to room E4.

"There's a door," Ruthie said, and they stepped through the wooden structure to the back wall of the room. They listened for a few moments before turning the brass doorknob. The hinges were on their side, so the door opened toward them, making it easier to peek into the room. It was Saturday morning and the museum hadn't filled up yet; the coast was clear and they went in.

Directly in front of them was a tall painted folding screen, useful if they had to duck out of sight fast. The walls of this room were of very dark stained wood— almost black—with ornate carvings of plants and birds and vines. Intricate detailing and gilding covered almost every surface, from the chairs and cabinets to the chandelier hanging in the center of the room. Even the ceiling was decorated with carvings of flowers and fruit. A portrait of a man with a horse hung above the yellow marble fireplace, and a grandfather clock stood in the corner.

The air in the room felt as though it had been warmed by sunlight. That was the first sign that the room was alive. The second was the bird's nest they saw in a tree outside the window. A mother bird arrived with a wiggly worm in her beak just as they approached the window.

The view was long and green. The tree with the nest stood just past a patio and beyond it stretched a long grassy path, with trimmed shrubbery on either side. A very large house sat in the distance at the end of the lawn. Ruthie wondered what year it was out there.

"Let's check all the drawers to see if there's a clue— maybe something that might go with the ring. A jewelry box, or some kind of design that matches it," Jack suggested.

"I'll take this side of the room—you do that side, okay?"

While Jack checked in the drawers of the large secretary between the windows Ruthie went straight for a chest of drawers across the room. It stood on curvy carved legs and was made of a kind of wood that had swirls like marble. She opened each one of its thirteen drawers.

Empty.

She looked around the room for anything that might help them figure out where the ring came from and how it had ended up in A2. She scrutinized the pattern on the rug but nothing stood out. She inspected the inlay in the furniture. Her eyes scanned the patterned surfaces, searching for some element that might lead them in the right direction.

Ruthie crossed over to a small table next to the fireplace. Its one drawer turned out to be empty, but there were two books lying on the table. She lifted them up and discovered they were fakes, props made for the room—they didn't open at all. Her gaze drifted toward the fireplace and something caught her eye. The cast-iron grate for holding wood had a carving on it. It was sooty and hard to make out at first, as it blended in with the charred blackness of the fireplace, but she saw on it a design that looked similar to the center of the ring. And worked into the decoration was a date: 1687.

"Jack! Bring the ring over here."

"Awesome," he responded as soon as he focused on what she was pointing at.

"I know. I bet that's the year out there. The catalogue said the real Belton House was built between 1685 and 1689," Ruthie added.

"The design is almost the same as the ring."

Ruthie put the ring in her messenger bag. Together, they headed straight for the other door in the room and crossed the threshold to the patio. The sun shone in a cloudless sky and its position overhead meant that it was about noon. A gentle breeze blew. Squirrels skittered across the lawn just past the patio. On their right they had a view up a gentle rise, toward a stately mansion.

But they couldn't see very far on the left, because the corner of the brick structure that was the Thorne Room, their portal, was in the way. They would have to leave the patio for a better view.

Ruthie didn't want to be seen in her modern clothes, but Jack was already off the patio. Still nervous about having been separated from him before, she followed.

After a few paces they reached the edge of the building and were no longer shielded by it. To the left they saw a village in the distance. But nearer to them a woman sat on a bench under a small stand of trees with a circle of children in front of her. They were reading silently, so Ruthie and Jack didn't notice them until it was too late. They were seen.

One of the smaller children, not attentive to her reading, spied them right away.

"Who are they?"

The woman also saw Ruthie and Jack. She looked them up and down, especially seeming to notice their shoes. In all of their time travels, the shoes were what stood out the most. But the woman reacted differently than all the others. She gave a quick gasp and put her hand to her face as if she didn't want to be seen. She turned away from them and stood up.

"Children! Come! Immediately!" she ordered, and rushed away in the direction of the large house.

"That was weird," Jack said.

"I know. That woman seemed . . . *scared* of us. How are we going to explore if we keep freaking people out? We need the right clothes." Ruthie bit her lip in thought. "The problem is, I don't think we'll find any clothes in this corridor."

"How do you know?"

"The first room is the church room. E1 is Christina's

room and we know it doesn't have a closet. Neither does E2. E3 is a fancy reception room and E5 is a kitchen."

They walked back to the patio.

"I know—the Wentworth room!" Jack said. "It's almost the same period. Those clothes will work!"

Ruthie brightened for a moment but then slumped. "I didn't bring the climbing chain. I didn't think we'd need it."

But Jack grinned. "I know how we can get there!"

···8···
THE OTHER WAY IN

"I CAN'T BELIEVE I SHOWED you this. Really?"

Ruthie was astonished as Jack led her to a small nook to the right of Gallery 11 that held a door. Less than a month ago they had gone back to the time of Jack's pirate ancestor and inadvertently changed the course of history, putting Jack's very existence in jeopardy. When that happened, an alternate version of Ruthie's life started seeping into her memory. In that other life, Ruthie had discovered a completely different way into the corridor behind the American rooms.

Because of the way the magic worked, Ruthie had no memory of any of this. But for some reason Jack did. The idea that in an alternate life she had already done it gave her no comfort at all. As Jack directed her under a door to the guard's locker room, across a short tiled expanse, and then under another door to the information booth,

Ruthie felt all the nervous jitters that she'd had the first few times they'd experienced the magic.

This part was tricky. A volunteer museum worker—a docent—always sat there, ready to answer questions for visitors. Ruthie and Jack peered out and up from under the door to the booth.

"We have to get to the floor vent over there." Jack pointed straight ahead to the far side of the booth. "That'll lead us to a duct that runs under the gallery and into the American corridor."

"You sure?"

"Positive. We did it before. When we get to the vent we'll squeeze through the grate. It's only a ten-foot drop or so. Like hanging from a ceiling and letting go."

"If you say so," Ruthie said. "How will we get back out?"

"I've got some nylon cord in my pocket."

Of course he does, Ruthie thought.

"We can knot it for climbing."

They shimmied out from under the door and started running. The vent was about five feet away (sixty feet to the tiny twosome). If the docent turned, or if someone came to the counter and looked past her, they would be seen.

When they were halfway to the vent, a man came to the counter to ask the docent a question. Ruthie and Jack could see him clearly, which meant they too could be seen by the man.

"Hey!" the man exclaimed as Ruthie looked way up

and made eye contact with him. "I think you've got . . . mice?"

They raced the rest of the way and reached the vent. The small squares of the grate were big enough that they could easily fit in. Ruthie copied Jack, who was already in up to his chest. She slid feetfirst as fast as she could down into the dark vent. She tried to hold on, but one hand slipped and she dangled.

"You can do it," Jack whispered.

In the dim light Ruthie saw him drop. She felt the vibrations of huge footsteps on the floor near the vent. She let go. Before her feet had hit the bottom she felt a beam of intense light hit her.

Jack grabbed her sleeve, yanking her deeper into the duct, away from the light.

"I don't know what that was," they heard the woman say. "Strangest-looking rodent I've ever seen!" The light clicked off.

"Now what?" Ruthie whispered.

"We follow the duct until we see the other end," he whispered back, adding, "I'm not going to turn on my flashlight, in case they could see the light through the vent."

Ruthie wasn't sure what was worse, hurtling forward without seeing anything at all or having Jack use his flashlight and find out what—if anything—might be lurking in the vicinity.

Adrenaline propelled her through the suffocating

dark. Finally, the faintest checkerboard glow appeared overhead.

They stood directly under the grate, looking up. It was about ten feet high. Jack unwound a skein of cord from one of his large lower pockets.

"What else do you have in there?" Ruthie asked.

"Just a couple of S-hooks and my Swiss Army knife."

The cord itself was only slightly bigger in circumference than a toothpick.

"Will that hold us?" she asked skeptically.

"It's deep-sea fishing cord. It's strong enough if we go one at a time."

"But it's too skinny to grab hold of," Ruthie said. Even if it didn't break, she didn't see how they could climb it.

"I see what you mean," Jack said, chewing the inside of his cheek. "I was kind of picturing it in its full size with us small."

"And how are we going to attach it?" The S-hooks in his pocket were now far too small to hook on to the metal grate. The thought of being stuck in that duct, with no way to get out, hit Ruthie like an icy wave. She imagined what would happen if they yelled for help. Would anyone hear their tiny voices, buried deep under the carpeted floorboards? And if they were rescued in their miniature state, what would happen next?

"I have an idea," Jack said at last. "Maybe this will work."

He knotted the cord, creating loops similar to those of the crochet chain. But the loops were at bigger intervals and large enough to grab hold of and stick a foot into. When he finished, the cord had about five loop "handles."

"This type of knot gets tighter when you put weight on it," he explained, pulling on a loop.

"But we can't reach the grate to hang it," Ruthie pointed out.

Jack took off a shoe. He tied one long unknotted end of the cord to it. He handed the shoe to Ruthie and then got down on his hands and knees. "Climb on my back and lob it through a few times to wrap it around the crosspieces."

"All right." Ruthie stepped gently on his horizontal back, balanced herself, and tossed the tiny shoe into a square in the grate. It fell back through another square and hung down to about the level of her waist. She repeated the action eight or nine times and then gave the looped part a good tug. "That should do it."

"You go first," Jack said, still on his hands and knees. "I'll come up after."

Ruthie grabbed hold of a loop that was above her head, almost at the grate, and lifted her feet up and into another. The cord was so thin it dug into her hand and she was glad the distance was so short. In two steps she was close enough to grab the grate and pull herself up into the American corridor. She watched through the squares, making sure that the cord didn't slip from the grate, while Jack climbed up.

"Made it!" he crowed as he clambered out. He reached

down for his shoe, which was still dangling from the cord, just below the top. "Pretty good idea, huh?"

"Not bad," Ruthie admitted.

Jack unwound the cord and let it fall to the base of the vent.

"When we come back we can just drop down. But we're going to need it to climb out at the other end."

Getting the eighteenth-century clothing was a cinch, but when they stood ready to go back through the duct, Ruthie noticed a small problem. "We can't make this climb *and* hold on to the clothes. We need to put them on."

They slipped the heavy fabrics over their own clothes. Racing through the dark passage, Ruthie thought once again how beautiful but ridiculous the women's clothing of this earlier time was. Wearing all these layers would put anyone at a disadvantage.

"When you get out there, don't wait for me—just run to the door, okay?" Jack said.

"Okay," she said. "What about your shoe?"

"I'll figure something out."

She hoisted herself up from the looped cord and stuck her head out. The docent was sitting on her chair, reading. Ruthie heaved herself, dress and all, the rest of the way through the grate and ran to the door leading to the guards' locker room. She hadn't counted on how much tighter the squeeze would be with the voluminous dress, but she tucked it all in under the door and waited.

And waited.

He was taking too long.

What if something had happened? What if he had been wrong about the strength of the cord? Jack weighed a few pounds more than Ruthie—what if the cord had snapped this time? Or worse, what if a cockroach had found him? All he had was his Swiss Army knife, which, shrunken, would be no use whatsoever against such a giant and naturally armed beast. Or perhaps he was stuck in another spiderweb!

She was about to run back when she saw Jack's head pop up through the grate, his shoe in his mouth.

Ruthie looked toward the counter. The docent was still reading intently. Jack made a break for it, running unevenly with only one shoe on. He skidded to the door like it was home plate.

"What took you so long?" Ruthie asked on the other side.

"It was really hard to get my shoe untied with one hand. I grabbed it with my mouth so it wouldn't fall when I got it freed. Glad it was my own shoe!" he joked, wrinkling his nose.

Just then they heard a loud noise. They were standing next to the end of a long wall of lockers and the sound was the metal-on-metal clank of a locker slamming shut.

The two instinctively froze. After a second, Ruthie forced herself to lean forward and peek around the corner. Jack did the same. Down the row of full-size lockers, a single guard stood buttoning his uniform sweater. The locker next to them was open a crack. They had the same thought: before the guard had finished they were up and in.

A sweater hung from hooks high above them. On the locker floor sat a lunch box and a large metal thermos. Ruthie looked up at the giant cylinder, the letters spelling out the brand name as big as her and Jack. They waited, listening to the muffled and rhythmic sound of soft soles on the floor coming close. Soon the guard's giant shoes were just a yard away. Through the crack in the door Ruthie saw that they were the gummy crepe-soled type, which looked particularly lumpy up close; all the crevices were filled with chunks of dirt and dried mud, and the scuffs on the shoe leather were like abstract graffiti. Ragged ropes hung from the frayed bottoms of his khakis.

In a couple of seconds he stopped right in front of them.

Ruthie and Jack squeezed into the small space behind the lunch box. The locker door shut with a heavy metallic thud. The footsteps faded away, and they heard the information booth door opening and the thump of it closing.

"Oh, boy," Jack said, looking way up to the latch that now trapped them. Their eyes adjusted to the small amount of light coming through the ventilation slats high up on the door.

The locking mechanism consisted of two long metal poles that fed into holes at the top and bottom of the locker and met in the middle, where the handle was. When someone turned the handle, the bottom rod would rise up and the upper rod would pull down, releasing them from the holes. Simple—but impossible to make happen if you were only five inches tall.

"I'm going to have to grow to get us out," Ruthie decided.

"Let's hope we don't need a combination!" Jack said, his voice strained with worry.

Ruthie took the key from her pocket and dropped it.

In seconds Jack was knocked to the corner and buried under the fabric of Ruthie's long eighteenth-century dress. Ruthie found herself scrunched against the sweater, her head hitting the clothes hooks that hung down.

"Ouch!" she exclaimed. She tried to get in a better position to unlock the door. A part of the handle that connected to the rods stuck out a couple of inches. Ruthie grabbed it and pulled down. It didn't budge.

"It's not opening!"

"Try harder," Jack shrieked from under the fabric.

"I'm going to try to break it," Ruthie said, maneuvering down in the tight column of space. Finally she managed to grab the top of the thermos, sliding it up as high as she could. With a mighty whack she brought it down on the handle. The lock broke and the door burst open. The thermos went flying and so did she. She hit the ground but didn't see Jack anywhere! Had she crushed him?

"Jack! Where are you?"

After a few beats a rustling began and a small lump moved under the heavy garment near her feet.

"Sorry!" she said, lifting it off poor Jack.

"That was a rough ride!" he gasped.

"We'd better get out of here before someone comes in!"

Ruthie quickly put the thermos back in the damaged locker. She found the key on the floor and picked it up to shrink. Once she was small again, Ruthie held the heavy skirt above her feet and they ran to the exit, slid under the door, and came out in the small nook, where they took off the period garments. No one was around, so Ruthie dropped the key and they grew back to full size, leaving the outfits tiny. Jack grabbed the key and they ambled leisurely back to Gallery 11 as though nothing had happened. With the clothes in their pockets, they were ready to face whatever 1687 had in store for them. Would the mystery ring from Belton House help them discover who had possessed the key?

9

THE GOVERNESS

WHAT—OR WHO—COULD BE *out there?* Ruthie wondered as they looked out from the patio. Would they find any more clues about how the ring had found its way into the wooden box? Mrs. Thorne's letter said the key had to be reunited with a different box—a looking-glass box. Maybe someone out there could help.

Ruthie held the ring in front of her, letting it catch the sunlight, the flickering points of light bouncing off the gemstones like little warning flares, making Ruthie worry—perhaps she and Jack were not practicing enough caution. But something told her that searching for answers was not optional. They *had* to.

"Tell me what you know about this time," Ruthie said as she put the ring back in her bag.

"Not that much about England. But the Jamestown colony was already set up in Virginia. If anyone asks, we can say we're from there. Come on. We're wasting time," Jack said, his voice untroubled by worries. He skipped down to the grassy lawn.

They approached the road and turned toward the village. The buildings were small and snugly nestled together on either side of the road. Made of smooth white plaster between dark timbers that framed the structures, they stood one or two stories high with thatched roofs. The windows had small diamond-shaped panes. Ruthie thought they looked like fairy-tale houses.

Hand-painted signs hung above the doors to several of the shops. They saw a butcher shop, a cheese monger, and a shoe store—which had a sign calling it a cobbler shop. The time travelers blended right in with the villagers, and Jack was comfortable enough to ask a lady directions.

"Belton House? 'Tis the grand house atop the rise. Take High Road."

The route was easy, and in ten minutes they arrived at a graveled area that would today be called the driveway.

Belton House stood in the middle of a broad green lawn, dotted with beds of blooming rosebushes and tidy hedges. Ruthie thought about how the real E4—the one Mrs. Thorne copied—was actually in there, and she wondered what the other rooms might look like.

"Look," Jack said, pointing down the sloping lawn, away from the house. "There's our portal over there. We walked in a circle."

Ruthie felt a small rush of comfort seeing that, but

it was interrupted a few seconds later by an object that whizzed right between her head and Jack's.

"Duck!" Jack yelped.

They hit the ground just as another projectile hurtled by. This time Ruthie saw what it was—an arrow!

She started in the direction of the hedge, fearing that they had walked right into some sort of battle, when they heard peals of laughter.

Out of nowhere, two girls came running toward them. Ruthie thought they might be from the group they'd seen reading earlier, although she wasn't positive. The older one looked about their age. "Are you hurt?" she asked.

Ruthie and Jack stood up.

"No, we're fine," Jack answered.

"That was my brother William's doing! The scoundrel!"

Right on cue, the young scoundrel came forward, bow in hand, still laughing. Equipped with a half-full quiver strapped to his back, he appeared to be about eight years old.

"See, Margaret—no harm done!" the young boy said.

"You're impossible," his sister said, and grabbed the bow from him. Then she gave a curtsy. "I'm Margaret Brownlow. This is Rose," she said, nodding to the little girl hiding behind her, who looked about five years old.

Ruthie suppressed an urge to grin too widely at hearing the name of the family they were looking for and instead smiled politely. "I'm Ruthie Stewart, and this is Jack Tucker."

"And this is my brother William. We were having archery lessons, and it seems he decided to choose another target." She swatted him. "You might have killed them!"

"I'm going to tell Rivy!" the little girl named Rose said, and ran off to the house.

"No, Rose. Don't bother her. She's not feeling well," Margaret called after her. But the young girl didn't stop, disappearing into the house. Margaret turned back to Ruthie and Jack. "Please forgive my brother."

"That's o—" Ruthie began, but remembered that no one in this century had heard the word *okay*, so she corrected herself. "That's all right."

"Did we not see you earlier, down in the park over there?" Margaret asked.

"Possibly," Ruthie answered, and then changed the subject. "Do you live here?"

"Yes, we do."

"But you don't," William said. "I see by your manner."

"We're from the Jamestown colony," Jack responded.

William's jaw fell open like a wide-mouth jar.

"What brings you to Lincolnshire?" Margaret asked.

"Jack's here for an education, and I'm accompanying him," Ruthie said, remembering how rarely girls were educated in past times.

"Are there wild animals there?" William asked eagerly. "Do you fight the Indians?"

"We try to get along with them, since they were there

first," Jack explained, although he knew that period of history was filled with bloody clashes between the colonists and the Native Americans. "We use bows and arrows all the time for hunting," he added as a flourish.

"How's your aim?" William asked.

"I'm pretty good," Jack boasted.

William grabbed the bow back from his sister. "Show me." He motioned for Jack to follow him. Ruthie and Margaret exchanged looks and silently decided it would be best to join them rather than risk being hit by a stray arrow.

William led the way to their archery range, close enough to the house to see inside the tall windows. Ruthie thought she saw someone looking out at them, but there was glare from the sun, so she couldn't be sure.

Three more quivers and bows lay strewn about, as the lesson had been interrupted by Ruthie and Jack's arrival. Several yards away, a sheet with painted concentric circles hung in the middle of a large bale of hay that stood as a target.

Ruthie had taken archery last summer at camp. She didn't know where Jack had learned, but he seemed to be right at home. He inspected the bow, made sure the arrow was true, and checked the fletching on the end.

He took the proper stance and placed the arrow on the rest, then aimed and drew the string. The arrow cut the air, arcing nicely, and hit the target close to the bull's-eye with a satisfying thwack.

"Jolly good!" William complimented.

"I say—who've we here?"

Ruthie and Jack turned to see an older boy, maybe sixteen years old, coming toward them from a side garden. He held a book.

"Peter, this is Jack and Ruthie," William said. "From America!"

"America? In truth?" He approached them, his hand out to shake Jack's. Then he took Ruthie's hand and kissed it. Ruthie felt the blood rush to her face. "What brings you to Belton House?"

"Uh . . ." Ruthie told herself to get a grip. She felt in her bag and brought out the ring. "We found this. Does it belong to your family?"

"Can't say for certain," the older boy said, examining the ring in the sunlight. "Looks similar to our crest."

Margaret looked at it as well and handed it back to Ruthie. "Father hasn't mentioned anything missing."

A commotion rang out toward the house. Ruthie looked over and saw Rose holding a woman by the arm and pulling her through the doorway, wailing that William was "going to murder a boy and a girl"! The woman was the same woman they had seen reading with the children earlier. She was resisting.

"All's well, Rivy," Peter called over. "We have visitors—from America!"

At this, the woman fainted.

. . .

It was eerie sitting in the drawing room of Belton House. It was almost identical to Mrs. Thorne's version—the door to which was just down the road at the moment—but with some different furniture and paintings on the walls. And of course there was a real fourth wall, instead of the viewing window. The children had guided the woman here over her protestations that she was fine.

"A little light-headed—I should have had a larger meal, that's all," she said. But Peter insisted they all have tea and "biscuits," which were really cookies as far as Ruthie could tell.

Rose introduced the woman as Rivy, their governess. "She looked after our father and now she looks after us!" Rivy sipped her tea, and Ruthie heard a slight rattle of the teacup on the saucer.

They talked for some time, although the governess said little and attended mainly to Rose. Ruthie and Jack learned that the parents had gone to London for the "social season" and that children never went along until they were of an age to be seeking a marriage partner.

Rivy seemed to be a combination of nanny and teacher. Rose sat like a kitten curled up on the sofa next to her and stared at Jack's shoes. Ruthie made sure her own were covered by the long dress—finally a benefit to all that fabric.

At last the little girl couldn't contain herself, and she jumped up and skipped across the rug to get a closer look at Jack's sneakers. She poked them with a finger, as if they were hot.

"Why do you wear such ugly shoes?" she asked.

"Rose! That is unbecoming!" Margaret chided.

Jack laughed. "They're the kind of shoes we have where we come from."

"I think it's time you all headed back outdoors and finished archery practice." The governess stood up, not the least bit wobbly, and guided Rose away from Jack's shoes and toward the door. "I'll join you all in a bit."

The younger children led the way.

"Good book?" Jack asked, falling into step with Peter.

"Indeed! Riveting, I should say!" He held the book up for Jack to see. "*Gulliver's Travels.* Just published."

"That's a great story," Jack agreed. "Can I take a look?"

Ruthie noticed a slight frown on Jack's face as he thumbed through the first pages. But it disappeared as soon as they neared the bows and arrows and he handed the book back to Peter.

Rose brought a bow over for Ruthie. "Are you an archer too?"

"Not really." Ruthie took the bow. "But I'll give it a try." She stood in place and launched her arrow. It struck the target—not as good a shot as Jack's, but respectable.

"Watch me!" William stepped up and nudged Ruthie out of the way. His arrow landed right next to hers. "Bit of a breeze," he complained. "I'll give it another go." Which he did, and no one argued with him about grabbing another turn. This time his arrow landed closer to the bull's-eye and he gave a loud whoop.

They all took turns, even Rose, whose arrows hit the target because she was allowed to stand several feet closer.

While the arrows flew, Ruthie thought about the ring and what they should do with it: leave it here or take it with them. She felt that nagging notion about unintended consequences again. Would bringing this ring back in time cause history to change? Somehow the ring had arrived in the twenty-first century as a true antique. It had been carried through the centuries one year at a time and didn't appear to be a treasured valuable that the Brownlow family had been missing. They didn't seem to care about it one way or the other. And if they left the ring here, Ruthie mulled, it would be that much harder to find out what it had been doing in a box in the Wentworth room. She was deep in thought when she heard Jack talking to her.

"Don't you think it's time to go? It's getting late."

"Oh, right. We should. And, Jack," she said in a low voice, "I think we should keep the ring. I'll explain later."

"Won't you dine with us?" Rose implored when they said they must leave.

"I'm sorry. We really can't stay," Ruthie answered.

They said their goodbyes and the Brownlow children graciously invited them to make a return visit.

They began to walk back in the direction of the patio portal. Halfway there, Ruthie stopped.

"My messenger bag! I left it inside. The key and the ring are in it!"

They hurried back to the house. The children had already gone indoors. They knocked repeatedly but no one came. Jack tried the door. It was unlocked.

Feeling sneaky—but needing the bag—they tiptoed into the room. Ruthie went directly to the chair she'd been sitting on. It wasn't there!

They scanned the room. Just then one of the interior doors opened and the governess entered. She caught her breath when she saw them.

"You must be looking for your bag—I'll fetch it straight-away. Please wait here."

In a few minutes she returned carrying the bag. "Here it is. I found it and put it in a safe place."

Relief washed over Ruthie. "Thank you!"

"Safe travels," the woman said, and gave them a long look. "Perhaps we'll meet again."

On the way back to the patio, Ruthie told Jack about her thoughts on keeping the ring after all.

They passed through the portal and reentered the drawing room, seamlessly crossing the ocean of time to the miniature museum version in twenty-first-century Chicago. They didn't have enough time to take the clothes back to the Wentworth room, so they hid them behind the folding screen.

Out on the ledge, just before Ruthie tossed the key to the floor and jumped, Jack paused.

"Something's bugging me."

"What?" Ruthie asked.

"We thought we were in 1687, right?"

"That was the date on the fireplace grate and the catalogue said that Belton House was finished about that time," Ruthie answered.

"*Gulliver's Travels* was published in 1726!"

10

HINTS

RUTHIE COULD ALWAYS COUNT ON waking up at dawn—or before—whenever something was bothering her. She tried to stay asleep, burrowing her head into her pillow, but it was no use. She sat up in bed. The clock flashed 4:30.

Why couldn't she let these exciting adventures be just that? Why must she always overthink it? she asked herself. Ruthie was confident that Jack was snoring away at home, even though he'd done the very same things she'd done.

Time. Ruthie was preoccupied by *time*. Twice now the rooms had opened to a different era than they had expected. Jack had double-checked the publication date of *Gulliver's Travels* and found he was correct—1726. That was nearly forty years later than the period of the room. *Why?* And what was the three-hundred-year-old Brownlow ring doing in the box in the Wentworth room? How long had it been there? And who had put it there?

It was as though she were watching a movie and images—hints—had flashed across the screen so fast she hadn't consciously noticed them, but she'd seen them nevertheless. Those hints kept her awake.

And now they had the letter written by Narcissa Thorne herself, containing an ominous warning about the magic. The key belonged not with Ruthie, Jack, Mrs. McVittie, or anyone else, but in a box in a vault in California. In 1939!

Ruthie got up, took her messenger bag, and tiptoed into the living room, curling up in her dad's favorite reading chair. She turned on the lamp next to it and took the letter from her bag to read it again. These words prickled her nerves:

This is a most serious—dare I say dangerous—matter, as the key must be returned to its proper place in the looking-glass box. Do not try to search for the box; I have taken it with me to Santa Barbara, where it is secure in my vault.

She put the letter back and fished out the two rings. The incandescent light hit the gold and gemstones of the Brownlow ring, showing its age again. Yesterday—for a few hours—it had been brand-new.

She looked at the mood ring now. Its cheap metal was dull and lifeless. How had two rings of such contrasting value become paired? Under the light, she saw the color of the man-made gem change in her hand, from pale blue to a mucky yellowish gray. She had a hunch what mood that indicated.

She heard a noise and quickly threw the rings back in her bag. She snatched a magazine from the coffee table and flipped to the middle. But the sound was just a far-off garbage truck starting the day. *No need to be so jumpy,* she told herself.

Her toss had propelled the rings deep into the bag. Rummaging for them again, she saw something.

Not the rings. Not the letter. Something else.

It was a tattered piece of paper about one inch wide by three inches long. The printing was faded and difficult to read because it had worn off in the creased places. She saw the logo for the Field Museum of Chicago on the top and below that the words

THE TREASURES OF TUTANKHAMUN
June 16, 1977
Student $2.00

A ticket stub from 1977? Ruthie rubbed her eyes. Was she dreaming? *How did this get in my bag?* she wondered.

She took her phone out and texted Jack: Did u put smthng in my mssnger bag?

In a few minutes her phone buzzed: ASLEEP!!! Y rnt u?

She sighed heavily and put her phone away. Her thoughts were foggy. Looking at the ticket stub, she felt a shiver down the back of her neck. *Why am I not asleep? This is why.*

Ruthie was on her third caramel of the morning, hoping the sugar would give her a burst of energy. When they took a break at lunchtime, she brought out the ticket stub to show Jack and Mrs. McVittie.

"I remember the exhibition—the first big museum blockbuster, they called it," Mrs. McVittie reminisced.

Jack examined the stub. "Remember the ad we saw in the old newspaper? Weird!"

"I know. Weird is right," Ruthie said. "My bag was in my room all day yesterday. I had it with me the whole time on Saturday except for twice: once when we snuck into the American corridor through the information booth, and . . ." She stopped talking and stared at Jack, who was already staring at her.

"What is it?" Mrs. McVittie asked.

They began to recount their visit to Belton House and meeting the Brownlow children and their governess. They jumped on each other's words and jumbled up the order, they were speaking in such a frenzy. But Mrs. McVittie got the point.

"So the only time your bag was out of your possession was when you were shooting arrows in the garden?"

Ruthie nodded. "And then the governess brought it back for me when we went to look for it."

"What year did you say that was?" Mrs. McVittie asked.

"That's the other thing," Jack said. "We thought it was 1687, but it had to be at least 1726, the year that *Gulliver's*

Travels was published. One of the brothers—Peter—was reading it and said it had just come out."

"That's much later than the catalogue dates the room," Ruthie added.

The three fell silent.

Finally Ruthie spoke. "This could be too crazy, but . . . suppose the governess put it in my bag because someone before us went back to that time and gave it to her? And she had some feeling that we were like that earlier visitor and wanted to test us? You know, give us a signal."

"And she didn't want to come right out and tell us that she'd met someone from the future because that would sound nuts," Jack added.

"Right!"

"It's possible," Mrs. McVittie said.

"There's another possibility," Jack said slowly. "But it's even crazier."

"What?"

"Hang on." He jumped up and ran to the storeroom. He came back with one of the pages of interesting articles that he'd been saving from the packing newspapers. He didn't say anything, but held the item out for them to see.

"The King Tut exhibition," Ruthie said.

"I was saving this for the ad, but look what's on the other side!"

Ruthie remembered the story and the chill it had produced.

"'The case of the missing teen has reached a dead

end, police investigators said Friday,'" Mrs. McVittie read aloud. " 'Two weeks have passed since the disappearance of Becky Brown, and officials in Cook County are baffled. "There is scant evidence to go on," Detective Riley said at a news conference. "The only witness is the girl's seven-year-old brother, Oliver Brown. His testimony has been deemed unreliable due to his age. There is no evidence of an abduction. We are going to treat this as a runaway." Authorities insist the public should not be concerned that there is a criminal on the loose.'" When she finished she sat back in her chair and put her glasses down.

Ruthie put her hand to her mouth. "You don't think . . . could the governess know something about the missing girl?"

Bright and early the next morning they rushed to the museum to take another trip back in time to Belton House. The first thing they saw in Gallery 11 was a maintenance man chatting with the docent at the information booth.

"There were at least two of them, I'm certain," the woman replied.

"We'll check next week and see if the traps caught the little varmints," the man told her. "Have a good one."

Ruthie and Jack understood that they were the little varmints!

They took their time, blending into the crowd, before drifting to the alcove to use the magic key. When a family group went up to the booth, blocking the docent's view of the alcove, Jack retrieved the key from his pocket and let it work.

Usually the feeling of the magic flooding into Ruthie's hand was an overpowering sensation. But today was different. Her head was filled with questions—questions so pressing they seemed to have a physical presence—and as the magic breeze blew around them, these questions swirled around her. She and Jack shrank to the floor, but the questions loomed large.

Inside the small, dark section of corridor, they set up the toothpick ladder and made the climb. On the way up, Ruthie pondered what they should say to the governess. How would they ask her about a girl from the future who'd gone missing? Could this woman be connected to the key? Their theory was so far-fetched they might have it all wrong. Perhaps someone had bumped into Ruthie or brushed by her—in the museum, on a crowded bus—and the ticket stub could have fallen into her bag. Or maybe it had been stuck to something else that had made its way into her bag, such as a library book, for instance. And it had been a while since she'd cleaned out the bag—there was all kinds of junk at the bottom. It could have been there for weeks. Was she just trying to create a mystery where none existed?

Ruthie and Jack reached the top and made their way into E4. They found the eighteenth-century outfits where they'd left them in a heap behind the folding screen. They slipped them over their own clothes and went out to the patio. From the position of the sun it appeared to be mid-morning. Ruthie briefly thought about the ring dial and Freddy and smiled.

"It's weird to think we could maybe find Freddy through this room. It takes us to almost the same time as his room," Ruthie observed.

"Buckinghamshire would probably be a three- or four-day trip from here on horseback," Jack pointed out.

"How do you know that?"

"I was thinking the same thing last night. I looked up the distance," he answered. "It's cool to think about. I wonder if you could do that in any of the other rooms."

"Go in one room, come out another," Ruthie mused, and fell silent.

Halfway up the road to Belton House she turned to Jack and said, "We'd better plan what we're going to say. We can't just ask her about the missing girl."

"We'll ask her if she's ever heard of King Tut. You know, like it's an interesting story from history that we've studied. If she has something she wants to tell us, that'll be a signal."

"But what if she doesn't pick up on it?"

"Then probably we're on a wild-goose chase."

Ruthie considered that possibility. But her gut told her they were on the right track.

Approaching the house, they saw no one outside. This time they walked up to the front door, not the side garden door that they had used before. A heavy brass ring served as a door knocker, and Ruthie gave it a few strong raps. When no one opened it, Jack reached up and repeated the knock. He had barely taken his hand off the ring when the door opened. A towering, stern-looking man in dress clothes stood looking down at them over his long and angular nose.

"Yes?"

"We're here to see the governess," Ruthie said.

The man said nothing and closed the door.

"Does that mean we just wait?" Jack wondered.

Ruthie shrugged. "I guess so."

It wasn't too long until the door opened again. This time the governess stood before them. She smiled and asked them in.

"I'm sorry, but the children are out riding this morning. You're welcome to stay until their return."

"Actually . . . ," Ruthie began, but then thought better of saying they had come to see her. "That would be nice, Ms. . . ."

"Please, call me Rivy, as the children do."

They followed her down a marble-floored hallway into the drawing room. Along the way, Rivy asked a maid to bring them some tea.

"So," Jack asked when the three had sat down, "what do you teach?"

"I teach the basics of reading, writing, and arithmetic. A tutor comes for Peter, who is now advanced."

"How about history?" Ruthie asked.

"Yes. We study ancient Greece and Rome," she replied.

"Do you teach about ancient Egypt?" Jack prodded.

A storm of worry glazed Rivy's eyes, and Ruthie knew they had hit on something. The governess got up and stared out the window for a few long moments. The maid entered with a tray, set it on a nearby table, and left. Everything was very quiet.

Rivy breathed deeply. "Let me tell you a story," she began. "Once there was a young girl, a little older than the two of you. She had a nice enough life, but she didn't like it. She wanted excitement and adventure. She wanted to feel appreciated, and she wanted, above all, her very own parents."

The part about wanting adventure sounded familiar to Ruthie; her urge to explore had brought them here.

Rivy turned to them. "Do you want to hear more?"

They nodded.

"You see, her parents had died when she was young and she was raised by an aunt and uncle. Her brother was only a baby at the time, and as he grew up he was very attached to her. So attached that she found it tiresome. Although she loved him, she wasn't always very nice to him. And then . . . he disappeared."

Rivy stopped talking, her lips pursed. "Tea?" she finally managed to say.

"Sure," Ruthie answered. This was not what they had been expecting at all. They had thought they might be hearing the story of a missing girl, not a disappearing brother.

The woman poured three cups and then said something even more perplexing. "Did someone send you here?"

"No," Jack said.

"Why did you want to tell us that story?" Ruthie asked.

"It's a story that has been in my head for almost as long as I can remember. When you asked me about Egypt . . ." She swallowed hard.

"I asked you because of this." Ruthie took the ticket stub from her bag.

The woman nodded. "When you visited the other day—travelers out of the blue in your very strange shoes—something told me I should give it to you, so I dropped it into your bag. I've carried that around for so many years. I remember where it came from . . . but I'm afraid you'll think I'm not quite sane."

"I think we can help you with that," Jack offered. "You asked if someone sent us here. We were going to ask you if someone, maybe a girl, visited you a long time ago and gave the ticket stub to you."

Rivy shook her head. She opened her mouth to speak but closed it before saying anything. Ruthie saw something close to fear in her eyes.

"But it has something to do with the story you just told us?" Ruthie proposed.

"Yes. They are parts of the same unanswerable riddle that haunts me."

And then Jack's great memory for details came into play. "Was the little brother in your story named Oliver?"

At first Ruthie wasn't sure where Jack was heading. But then she too remembered the name of the brother in the newspaper article—the boy who was too young to be a reliable witness.

Rivy looked as though lightning had flashed in her face. "Yes! That is my brother's name!"

"*Your* brother?" Ruthie asked. "We thought his sister was Becky Brown!"

"*I* am Becky Brown. My full name is Rebecca Brown. 'Rivy' is a British nickname for Rebecca given to me by the children."

It took a moment for Ruthie and Jack to catch up after this astonishing revelation. They thought Rivy might know something about the missing girl; instead, it turned out she *was* that missing girl.

"How did you know my brother's name?" Rivy asked.

"Why don't we tell you a story and you tell us what you think?" Jack suggested.

"Please!" she responded.

"Once upon a time," Jack started, his storyteller's gift in high gear, "there was a girl who lived in a place called Chicago. . . ."

Jack got up from his chair and walked around the room, spinning his tale and weaving all the threads as he spoke. He began with the King Tut exhibition at the Field Museum, in the year 1977. "But the girl was more interested in another museum—the Art Institute. She had made an amazing discovery about the enchanted rooms there. She'd found a magic key, and with that key she could enter the rooms." Jack paused for dramatic effect. "But she could also exit her life—and her time. And one day she left and never returned to Chicago."

Rivy hung on his every word, her cheeks suddenly wet with tears. Ruthie too sat listening in awe as Jack put all the details in place.

"Yes!" Rivy said through great gulps of air, wiping her eyes with a handkerchief. It took another cup of tea for her to be calm enough to speak. "I thought it had to be a dream because it's all . . . impossible! I couldn't tell anyone. Sometimes I even thought I might be insane or possessed. Are you sure I'm not dreaming now?"

"Positive," Jack answered, taking a seat again.

"Tell us everything you remember," Ruthie said gently.

Rivy set her teacup on the table. "I'm from . . . Chicago? It was so different than it is here. I had a younger brother named Oliver. Our parents died in a plane crash just after he was born—I think I must have been about eight. That part is very foggy. I haven't thought about airplanes in who knows how long. We don't . . . have them now." She shook her head in disbelief and Ruthie imagined a sky never marked with the thin white crisscross of contrails. "One summer day he begged me to take him to see the King Tut exhibition—I was often his babysitter because our aunt and uncle worked a lot. We went to the

Field Museum but I told him he also had to go to the Art Institute with me to see the Thorne Rooms."

"Did you already know about the magic?" Ruthie asked.

"Yes . . . yes, I did." Her hands—which had been clenched—finally rested in her lap while she told her story. "My aunt and uncle knew a man who worked at the museum and somehow had the key. I remember he said there was a legend that it held some kind of special power. No one believed that. We all thought it was simply a charm, like people put on bracelets. He gave it to me as a necklace, a pretty piece of jewelry. At the museum one day, by myself, I discovered that it really was *charmed*. Then, that day with Oliver, I made him come with me, to explore."

"Did you know the rooms were portals to the past?" Jack asked.

"Yes, I did. I discovered that by accident the second time I visited the rooms. I stayed a little longer and realized I heard sounds coming from outside. I remember it was a fancy English room with red walls and a checkerboard floor. I turned and saw a horse and carriage pass by the window." She sipped her tea. "And I remember . . . a ring."

Ruthie reached into her bag and took out both rings.

Recognition registered on Rivy's face. She pointed first to the mood ring. "I wore that one; just a fad at the time. But this one," she said picking up the real jewel, "this is what brought me here."

"How? Why?" Ruthie wanted to know.

"It was a family heirloom. My real family—the Browns—are descendants of the Brownlows; our name was simplified when the family came to the United States. When I discovered that Mrs. Thorne had copied a room from the Brownlow estate, I wanted to go there, back in time, to meet my ancestors! I thought it would be almost like having my parents again. What a silly girl I was!"

"I don't think that's silly at all," Jack said.

Ruthie remembered how much it had meant to him to meet his great-times-six grandfather. "But why did you decide to stay?" she asked.

"I didn't." Her eyes welled with tears again. "I was stranded."

··· 11 ···
TELLING STORIES

RUTHIE AND JACK LISTENED TO Rivy—the missing
Becky Brown—while she told her story of what had happened. Almost forty years earlier, when she was fifteen,
she brought her seven-year-old brother with her into the
past. They found themselves in late seventeenth-century
Lincolnshire, England.

"Oliver was acting like little boys sometimes do," she
explained. "He ran around and was impatient. First he
wanted my rings. I let him have the mood ring, but when
he was bored with that he wanted the antique one and the
key too. He wanted to carry all of them, and I finally gave
in and let him. Once he'd seen Belton House—this one,
not the miniature—he wanted to explore more rooms,
especially the castle rooms. I was growing short-tempered
with him and he ran off. When I went to look for him, the
door—the portal, as you call it—had disappeared, and . . .

I never saw him again." She blinked hard. "He never came back for me. Ever."

Ruthie shuddered. She remembered the feeling she'd had just a few days ago when Jack had removed the animator from room E6 and she was cut off from her life for all of fifteen minutes. What if he hadn't come back and she'd been *trapped*?

And then it occurred to Ruthie: "Jack—we never figured out what the animator is."

"The what?" Rivy asked.

"It's the object in the room that makes the outside world alive. So far the animators have been old, from the time the room represents," Jack answered. "Whatever it is, Oliver must have taken it. Probably without even knowing it."

"But that doesn't make sense," Ruthie pointed out, "because we're here now. The room is animated. And the portal didn't close behind us."

"Maybe he put it back," Jack said.

"But then the portal would have reappeared for her," Ruthie said. "Something doesn't add up." Ruthie felt a shiver at the possibility of an unexpected animator or rules they didn't understand.

"Could it be the ring?" Rivy asked.

"You had the ring with you when you first came to Belton House?" Jack asked.

"I think it was in Oliver's pocket."

"So far, all the animators we've discovered have had to

stay put in the rooms. If you move them from their place, the portal closes," Ruthie explained.

"Maybe the ring works differently; maybe you can come out into the past with it," Jack suggested. "If the ring is the animator, when Oliver went out to the corridor the portal would have closed up." Jack scratched his head. "Maybe he came back to get her, but he didn't have the ring anymore—"

"Because he'd left it in the box where we found it!" Ruthie interjected.

"Right. Room E4 would've been dead."

Ruthie jumped up and ran to the window. Suppose, as Jack said, the ring as animator behaved differently than the others; suppose the portal closed later, when they were farther away from it . . .

"What's wrong?" Jack asked.

"We were able to see Belton House from the patio; can we see the patio from here?" Ruthie said, looking through the glass panes.

Jack joined her at the window. "There it is—just past those trees at the bottom of the slope."

Through a grove of trees Ruthie glimpsed the small patio next to a brick structure, but her heart still thumped even after the reassuring sight of the portal.

Rivy came to the window. From this perspective the portal looked only slightly larger than a small brick shed, with one door but no windows. "I've never seen that before. It's been such a long time, but I don't believe that's what it looked like when I came through."

"Could we ask someone—maybe the maid—to come in here to see if she can see it?" Jack asked.

Rivy went to the near wall and pulled on a long embroidered cord. "This rings downstairs in the servants' quarters," she explained.

The maid arrived shortly. "Yes, ma'am?" she said with a curtsy.

"Daisy, please come over here, and tell us what you see," Rivy directed.

The maid crossed to the window, looking at Rivy and the visitors questioningly. "Why, I see the gardens and the lawn, beyond. Am I supposed to see something else?"

"Do you see a small brick structure down there, in that grove of trees?" Ruthie prompted.

Daisy looked and looked. "Can't say that I do. Only the lawn, and a small sliver of the road that leads to the village."

"Thank you, Daisy. That will be all," Rivy said.

"Yes, ma'am." The maid curtsied again and left.

"What does this mean?" Rivy asked Ruthie and Jack.

"It means you can see the portal because you're here by magic," Jack explained. "Only the three of us can see it."

"Be prepared, Rivy; if you've never been able to see it before, it may disappear when we leave," Ruthie added.

"You mean, if I want to go back, this may be my only chance? Can't you leave me the ring?"

Ruthie shook her head. "We're not sure why the room is alive now, but I have a feeling it's something about the key and the ring *combined.*"

She took the key out of her bag. The metal glinted like icicles in sun. When she held the ring and key side by side, the ring began to pulse light just like the key. The key would glow in a burst and then the ring would mimic it, flashing in the same irregular beat, as though it were some kind of magical Morse code. They actually seemed to be communicating with each other. A beautiful tinkling sound began from far away and increased until it filled every corner of the room. They all watched and listened for several minutes.

"We shouldn't separate them. We don't know what would happen," Ruthie pointed out.

"Will you take me down there?" Rivy asked. "Just for a look."

"Sure," Ruthie said.

They left Belton House through the garden door and walked past the roses and shrubs. "How did you become the governess here?" Ruthie asked.

"At first I believed that someone would come back for me. While I waited I lived on apples from orchards and snuck vegetables from gardens. I slept on the ground in places where no one would see me. Several days passed and I knew I had to have more to eat and a place to stay. After the shock of realizing that I might be stuck in this time for a while I thought about what I could do. There are very few professions for a young woman in this era.

"I worked in a nearby village as a cook and a maid. As time passed, first a few months, then a year, then two, I became accustomed to this world. Even though I was young, I was well educated for a girl in this time. I heard that the Brownlow family—*my family!*—was in need of a governess, so I wrote them a letter and they hired me. It was a long time ago; I was the governess for the father of the children you met. He grew up and married and had his own family. So I've been educating my own ancestors!"

"That's amazing," Jack said.

Rivy told them that since she never had children of her own, she could claim deep love and affection for all the Brownlows; they were, after all, family, in the mixed-up and inside-out way brought about by the time travel.

"But I missed my life—especially Oliver—frightfully. Slowly the pain lessened but it never went away. Over the years, I guess, I substituted this family for the one I had been missing. I love them very much."

They reached the edge of the property and the three steps that led up to the patio.

Rivy took a deep breath. "This is not how Oliver and I . . . arrived."

Ruthie reached out her hand, which Rivy clasped willingly.

They walked up the steps and across the slate tiles of the patio. The door was visible in front of them and Jack opened it a crack. Still standing in the English country-side, they peeked three centuries into the future, into the Thorne Room. No one was at the viewing window, so Jack slipped in first. In the doorway, Rivy turned and looked back up the hill to Belton House before

crossing the threshold into the world she'd left behind so long ago.

"It's almost the same, isn't it?" She gazed around the room. "That painting is different, and some of the furniture as well." Then she rushed over to the viewing window. "But that's not as I remember it at all. How odd."

"Better not stand there." Ruthie took her hand again to guide her away from the glass. "We might be seen."

They lingered for a minute or two, while Rivy made a 360-degree turn, taking it all in.

"Look at that kitten in front of the fireplace!" they heard a young voice squeal from the gallery, referring to the room right next to them.

"Quick! This way," Jack said.

They sped out the other door, through the framework, and into the corridor. As soon as she was through the framework Rivy stiffened.

"I know, the scale can make you dizzy. Don't look down," Ruthie said.

"It's not that. It's just . . . *completely* different. Is this some kind of trick?"

"No," Ruthie promised.

"I don't like this at all! Everything feels all muddled. Please, take me back."

"All right," Jack replied.

When the viewers in the gallery had moved on, the three returned to the room, Rivy going directly to the far door and passing back across time.

They rushed to keep up with her. Out on the patio she said haltingly, "I don't understand. . . ."

Ruthie reached out to stroke Rivy's forearm, not knowing what to say. This reaction was so unexpected, more than just the vertigo that she and Jack had felt when they first experienced the colossal scale in the corridor.

At last Rivy's breathing eased and she asked them how they had come to possess the ring. They explained about the box in the Wentworth room that contained the two rings. When they had finished, Rivy sighed. "I have so many more questions—I don't know where to begin. It's almost too much for me."

Ruthie wondered what was next. Moments ago she had *assumed* Rivy felt rescued and wanted to come back. But suddenly Ruthie wasn't so certain that Rivy would choose to return.

With tears in her eyes, Rivy asked, "Could you do me a favor?"

"Sure," Jack said.

"Do you think you could find Oliver? Or at least find out what happened—why he didn't come back for me?"

"We can try," Ruthie said. But the question implied that there was something big about the magic that Rivy might not understand. Ruthie had *assumed* Rivy knew this rule of how the magic worked, and once again she realized how mistaken assumptions can be.

Ruthie looked at Jack and could tell he was thinking the same thing: would Rivy have been so careless as to let a seven-year-old boy keep the key if she'd known how it worked? Ruthie imagined the young boy impulsively slipping away and out of the corridor, growing big once more and having no way to shrink again without his sister. She pictured a little boy alone in the museum, crying for his lost big sister.

Yes, Mrs. Thorne, Ruthie thought, *this is a most serious and dangerous matter.*

"I think we need to tell you something," Ruthie said.

"What is it?"

"The magic of the key . . . the shrinking part. Did you know it only makes girls shrink?"

She stared at them, not comprehending. "But . . ."

"Boys can shrink only if they are holding a girl's hand. And once a boy puts the key down—back out in the museum—he regrows," Jack explained.

"You mean . . ." She choked up again. Finally she said. "He *couldn't* come back for me."

They nodded.

"Then you must find him!"

When they arrived at the shop Mrs. McVittie had a client in the front room. Ruthie and Jack went to the storeroom to try to get some work done, but they were both too preoccupied.

"I can't stop thinking about the animator," Ruthie said, sitting on a box. "We have to find out if we are right about the key and the ring working together. If the ring was passed down in the Brown family, then that room would never have been alive until 1977, when Rivy—Becky Brown—walked into it with the ring and the key."

"That's possible," Jack said, nodding.

"And so far, all the other rooms have gone dead when we've moved the animator."

"Like the vase in E9; just picking it up shut the whole thing down."

"Right. But that didn't happen to Rivy and Oliver, and it didn't happen to us today. I have a hunch Mrs. Thorne left something else in there, so the room was alive when Rivy and Oliver visited. Something that's not there now—"

"Because Oliver pocketed it on his way out!" Jack completed Ruthie's thought.

"Exactly. And that's why the key and the ring flashed so much when we showed them to Rivy."

"Why?"

"I think they were showing us that finding Rivy was what they . . . *wanted* us to do; that was their job. They're not exactly animators, but they worked in place of one."

Jack nodded, mulling over the idea. "Let's see what they're doing now."

Ruthie took them from her bag and held them in her open palm while they watched and waited. The key and the ring glowed in a gentle, synchronized pulse. But the show they had seen in Belton House was over for the time being.

"It's like they're turned on but in power-saver mode,"

Jack said. "And another thing—did we arrive in 1726 because Rivy had been back in time for almost forty years?"

"That must be right," Ruthie said. "We know for sure that she went back in time starting in 1977; the math works."

The shop door closed and they rushed into the front room.

At the same time that Jack exclaimed, "We have to find a missing person!" Ruthie pronounced, "We found a missing person!"

"What happened?" Mrs. McVittie asked, having heard their conflicting statements. "What did you discover?" She made them sit and handed them each a wrapped sandwich from the deli.

"I don't know if I can eat," Ruthie said.

Jack unwrapped his sandwich without hesitating. Between bites, he began the story of going to find out something about the missing girl from the article and instead meeting that very girl. Only now she was in her fifties.

"She's lived practically her whole life in the wrong century," Ruthie added.

"She'd been handling it pretty well—her memories were getting clearer. But when she looked through the viewing glass and when we took her out in the corridor she seemed confused," Jack explained.

"Perhaps it could have something to do with the reinstallation," Mrs. McVittie suggested.

"The what?" Ruthie asked.

"Until the nineteen eighties the rooms were in a different part of the museum. It was a very dark and out-of-the-way space under a stairwell."

"I didn't know that," Ruthie said. "When were they moved?"

"I can't tell you precisely. But most of them were put in storage for a number of years. It's possible that when they were reinstalled, changes may have been made to the dioramas."

"So the corridor would have looked completely different in 1977? And the rooms wouldn't even have been in Gallery 11?" Jack asked.

"That's right," Mrs. McVittie said.

"We have to find her brother, Oliver Brown," Ruthie declared. "He must be in his forties now."

"You'll have to be very sensitive when you talk to him," Mrs. McVittie advised.

"I was thinking about that," Ruthie said. "I think we should ask Dr. Bell to help us."

Dr. Bell's childhood had been complicated not only by the loss of her mother when she was young but also by her visits to the rooms. The magic had produced thrilling adventures *and* destructive outcomes. She could guide them better than anyone.

"Good idea," Jack said. "He'll believe her; *I'd* believe her if I were in his place. We'll ask her to come with us."

Ruthie was finally able to take a small bite of sandwich. "*If* we find him."

· · · 12 · · ·
SLIPPERY STONES

"**WHO KNEW THERE WOULD BE** so many people named Oliver Brown?" Jack moaned. They were at Jack's house. Ruthie's parents and sister, Claire, were out of town for the summer-abroad orientation, so she would be staying there for the next two nights. They had searched the name and hundreds of links came up. "And we don't even know that he still lives around here. He could be in Alaska, or anywhere!"

"This might be impossible," Ruthie worried. Just like the rooms, the digital world provided an endless number of connections in time and space. How could they possibly sort through them all?

"Too bad we don't know his middle initial—that would narrow down some of the Oliver Browns. We could go back and ask Rivy."

"Birth announcements!" Jack exclaimed, typing in a new search.

After a few minutes he cried, "Bingo!"

Under a newspaper listing of births in Chicago on March 3, 1970, they read:

**OLIVER ZACHARY BROWN, A BOY,
WAS BORN TO MARJORIE AND ROBERT BROWN,
10:42 A.M., 8 LB., 2 OZ.
HE HAS A SISTER, REBECCA LILLY, AGE 8.**

When they limited their search to the Chicago area, there were five Oliver Z. Browns. They searched those five and came up with an amazing amount of information. They found a picture that showed one to be African American, so they were able to check him off the list. Ruthie sighed in relief as the list got shorter.

Of the four remaining, they discovered a teacher, a CEO, an artist, and an accountant. The artist was the next to check off the list. They found his website, where his biography stated that he was the oldest of six children.

The teacher was definitely too young. The CEO was at a corporate headquarters downtown, and they were able to find pictures of him as well. He was about the right age. He didn't look much like Rivy, but it wasn't out of the question they could be related. The accountant had an office in the South Loop, but they didn't find any pictures of him online, so he remained another possibility.

"Not bad for a couple of hours of research," Jack said.

"What are you two working on?" Lydia asked, popping her head into Jack's doorway. She had an extra pillow and blanket for Ruthie.

"Just following up some leads," Jack answered. "We've been finding out all kinds of stuff."

"For Mrs. McVittie?" Lydia asked.

Jack nodded noncommittally.

"It's been really interesting," Ruthie added, a touch of guilt creeping into her stomach; she knew they weren't exactly answering Lydia's questions. "Thanks for the blanket."

"Probably would be a good time to hit the sack. If you want a bedtime snack, there are oatmeal cookies in the kitchen."

Jack zoomed past the two of them and was pouring milk by the time Ruthie got there. Lydia headed back to her studio around the corner.

Jack dunked his cookie into his glass of milk and took a slurping bite. "You know," he said with a full mouth, "we should call Dr. Bell tomorrow."

Ruthie bit into the crispy-chewy round, still warm from the oven, and tried to imagine what they would say to Oliver Brown.

Dr. Bell picked Ruthie and Jack up at Mrs. McVittie's shop a little before noon on Thursday and drove them the short distance to Oliver Brown's office. They had decided that since the CEO didn't look like Rivy, they might as well try the accountant first. Dr. Bell had agreed to help them and had called his office to make an appointment for a time when she could get away from her office.

"It will be a delicate thing, meeting this man," Dr. Bell advised. "This is a very old and deep wound. You don't know how people will react."

Looking out the window, Ruthie thought about how Rivy had lived the majority of her life in the eighteenth century. Ruthie pondered the things Rivy had missed; besides historic events, she pictured things like birthdays, graduations, parties, and family trips, all the moments that make a life.

They arrived at a nondescript office building, all gray metal and glass. Inside, they read the wall directory: *Oliver Z. Brown Associates, 15th floor.*

The elevator opened to a long hallway, and the office they wanted was at the end. Dr. Bell opened the door and Ruthie and Jack followed her in.

A receptionist looked up from her computer. "May I help you?"

"Hello. I'm Dr. Caroline Bell and I have an appointment with Mr. Brown."

The receptionist rose. "This way, please."

When they entered his office, Oliver Brown stood to greet them. Ruthie wasn't sure they'd come to the right place. Did he look like Rivy? Maybe a little around the eyes. Rivy's hair had gone mostly gray; this man's was still dark.

Dr. Bell introduced herself and said that Ruthie and

Jack were friends who wanted to come along and learn a little of what accountants do. She kept her explanation simple and started by asking him about his qualifications as a way of finding out anything she could about him.

While they talked, Ruthie looked around the room for clues. The office was immaculate, with not a single piece of paper out of place. The walls were painted white, and the only decoration was a framed photo of the Chicago Water Tower. There were no family photos anywhere, not even of a pet dog or cat. He wore no wedding ring.

The shelves behind him held books on accounting and business, kept in place with plain metal bookends. Ruthie saw one unidentifiable greenish object, looking something like a small back scratcher, thin in the middle with two knobs on each end. On his desk sat a computer, an adding machine, a dozen perfectly sharpened pencils lined up, a brass paperweight in the shape of a pyramid, a letter opener, and an electric pencil sharpener.

Jack kicked Ruthie's foot subtly and with a glance directed her eyes to the pyramid. *Of course!*

When there was a pause in the discussion of the tax code, Jack jumped in. "Nice pyramid. Where'd you get it?"

"Oh, that? When I was a kid, there was this great exhibition at the Field Museum about King Tut. My sister took me and bought me this as a souvenir."

This time Ruthie's foot nudged Jack's—she could barely contain herself.

Dr. Bell caught the cue brilliantly. "My dad used

to work at the Art Institute. I spent a lot of time in that museum as a child."

Oliver Brown didn't respond but stared at the pyramid. He didn't offer it to Jack for closer inspection, which surprised Ruthie. It wasn't fragile, and most people would have let a kid take a closer look. But he picked it up as gently as if it were a crown jewel. He looked at it a little too long before he returned to tax talk.

When he set the pyramid back on the desk, Ruthie noted how precisely he did so, lining it up just right. Then he straightened a couple of pencils next to the letter opener.

The letter opener!

She hadn't noticed it at first, but it appeared to be something much finer than a museum souvenir. It looked like sterling silver, very old and out of place amid the drab items on the desk.

"That's a beautiful letter opener," Ruthie said, reaching for it. She saw him tense as she did so, but she went ahead and picked it up. "Where did you get it?" she asked.

"Um . . . I've always just had it. A family heirloom," he answered unconvincingly.

Ruthie looked at him, but he dropped his eyes. She went back to inspecting the object.

It was shaped like a miniature dagger or sword, like Excalibur from the King Arthur stories. The pointed blade reflected a steely gray light, and set in the center of the carved handle, where the guard crossed the hilt, a milky moonstone glowed iridescently. It was about nine inches long. She found the hallmarks and announced, "It's English sterling. Pretty old."

"Ruthie and Jack have summer jobs working for an antiques dealer," Dr. Bell explained.

"I'd say late seventeenth century. It reminds me of something—like I've seen it somewhere," Ruthie continued. Oliver Brown sat mutely, almost frozen.

"Are you all right?" Dr. Bell asked. "Can I get you some water?"

"P-perfectly fine," he stammered, and cleared his throat. "Now, where were we?"

Dr. Bell replied with something about tax deductions. Ruthie was trying to think of how to redirect him when she felt something warm on her leg. She had her messenger bag in her lap—the key and the rings inside— and heat began permeating the canvas, even the denim of her jeans. She reached in, but before she could find them, hot light was seeping through the fabric. With her right hand in the bag, touching the two pieces of metal, the letter opener in her left hand began warming even more, as though a circuit were being completed and she was the conduit.

Suddenly the old sterling silver erupted, emitting rays so intense they were impossible for Ruthie to conceal in her closed fist. She yanked her right hand from her bag, breaking the connection, and the letter opener—though still warm—quieted.

But it was too late. "What was that?" asked Oliver Brown.

The light show they had seen when Rivy held the key and the ring began again as soon as Ruthie took them from her bag.

Stunned, Oliver Brown stared at the flickers of light coming from the objects. "What is this . . . ?"

"Have you ever seen these before?" Ruthie held the key and the two rings closer to him so he could get a good look.

He shook his head, but he appeared to be looking right through the objects to a distant point.

"Are you sure?" Jack coaxed.

Oliver Brown's expression changed. He directed his focus on Dr. Bell as if to erase Jack and Ruthie from his field of vision. "Dr. Bell, I think we should set up another appointment. This . . . trick . . . is a distraction."

"Ruthie, maybe you should put those away for now," Dr. Bell said gently.

Oliver Brown stood up. His mouth was tight, and tiny beads of sweat formed on his upper lip.

Ruthie put the key and the rings in her bag and set the letter opener back on the desk, placing it exactly as it had been, its glow subsiding.

"Please ask my receptionist to reschedule," Oliver Brown said to Dr. Bell, still ignoring the fact that something strange had just taken place in his office.

"Certainly," she answered, rising. The three headed to the door, where Dr. Bell turned to him. "You know, I also had something in my office for many years—a beautiful antique silver box. I could barely remember where it came from. Ruthie and Jack helped me understand how I ended up with it."

He looked at her blankly. But Ruthie saw something like pain or sorrow cross his face for an instant. He turned his eyes to the floor.

They left the office and walked to the elevator without speaking.

"I wasn't expecting that," Jack said in the lobby.

"I should have gone alone. Or prepared you two better. I was afraid this might happen," Dr. Bell said.

They passed through the revolving doors and walked down the sidewalk, but as they turned the corner toward the parking lot they heard a shout.

"Wait! Wait! I'm sorry," he said breathlessly. "Is there someplace we can talk?"

Mrs. McVittie put the Closed sign in the front window of her shop. Before leaving to go back to her office, Dr. Bell told Oliver Brown her story of how she had learned about the magic as a little girl. Mrs. McVittie did the same. Mr. Brown seemed dazed, maybe even numb, but he listened to every word.

Ruthie and Jack explained how they had found the key and discovered the shrinking magic, but also what Dr. Bell and Mrs. McVittie had not: that the rooms were portals to times past. "So that's our story," Ruthie concluded. She had arrived at the point where they'd found the ring that led them to the Belton House room.

Oliver Brown said nothing. He held the pyramid and letter opener in each hand, knuckles white from his tight grip. He sat rigidly in his chair, like a stone pillar, in contrast to the sagging comfort of everything in the cozy shop.

Finally he leaned forward. "And did you go back in time through the Belton room? Did you meet someone . . . named Becky?"

"Yes," Ruthie answered.

He swallowed hard. "Is she . . . was she . . ."

"She's fine," Jack reassured him. "She asked us to find you."

Carefully, like crossing a swift river by stepping on slippery stones, they filled him in on Rivy's—Becky's—life. They didn't want to go too fast and risk upsetting him.

"It's been a long time," he said. "Almost forty years." Ruthie could see his posture slacken, his hands relaxing. "I remember how exciting the day had been. We went to see the King Tut show. I was seven years old, captivated by the mummies and the gold. Then Becky took me to the Art Institute. I can't quite remember what happened next; Becky told me to close my eyes and she grabbed my hand, I think. The next thing I knew, we were running in a huge, even darker place. We started climbing something that looked like giant pushpins stuck into the wall at intervals—handles to grab hold of and step on. It was difficult, and Becky told me not to look down."

"Cool idea!" Jack interjected.

"That led to some kind of scaffolding, which we

climbed like playground equipment. We made our way through a wooden framework and into very fancy rooms."

They spent a couple of hours listening as Oliver Brown remembered more and more about that day with his sister. He recalled quick visits to a few rooms, and pocketing a jade carving from one. "I still have that," he added, sounding apologetic. He had pestered Becky to see the fascinating objects she kept in her pocket: the old key, and the two rings. "I was especially interested in the mood ring," he explained.

They went to room E4, and then through a door and into an enclosed patio. He had no idea whatsoever that they had gone back in time. When they approached the real Belton House, he wasn't interested in a "boring old house" and ran off, back to the patio door and into the room. On the desk in the room he spied the letter opener, which he thought was a dagger. "I had to have it, so I grabbed it and ran out of the room," he told them.

Ruthie and Jack understood the significance of this; the letter opener was most certainly the animator. Ruthie jumped in. "Did you take anything else from that room?"

"That was the only thing," he answered defensively. "I promise. I poked my head in a few more rooms, fiddling with the mood ring all the while. Until I got bored with it and dropped it in a big wooden box in one of the rooms. I thought it looked like a jewelry box. I think I dropped the other ring in the box too."

Jack looked at Ruthie, and she gave him a subtle nod.

Oliver continued. "I ran around in the framework behind the rooms, trying to climb it like the monkey I was, while I waited for my sister. I remember standing on a very high ledge, looking down, and then . . ."

He choked up and for a moment couldn't speak.

"What?" Ruthie prompted.

"I dropped my sister's key to see how long it would take to reach the bottom. I didn't know it was magic. I remember hearing the clinking sound."

"Then what happened?" Jack asked.

"I waited and waited, and she never came back for me. I remember getting hungry and cold and tired. I managed to climb down the same way we had climbed up. Somehow I made my way under a door. I was crying by then. The museum was deserted, and it seemed so colossal. I was still tiny and I felt dizzy and utterly confused. What I remember is that somehow I just grew big again. It was terrifying."

"You poor child," Mrs. McVittie said.

"A guard found me crying for my sister. The police showed up, and I was asked all kinds of questions. I'm sure I made no sense at all."

"Did you ever try to go back?" Jack asked.

He sighed heavily. "I've been back hundreds of times, just to look at that room . . . hoping . . . I don't know what I expected would happen." He shook his head, and the deep line that had run across his forehead began to soften. "But tell me: if my sister is well . . . why didn't she ever come back?"

Ruthie had been dreading this: telling Oliver the reason she could not return.

She told him how she and Jack had stumbled on the key and its magic and gently explained how the shrinking works only if a girl holds the key.

"Your sister didn't know that either," Jack added quickly. "She also didn't know about the animators."

Oliver looked confused, and Jack explained that aspect of the magic. "They're the things that make the rooms portals to the past," Jack continued. "If that object is taken from the room, the portal closes. Until that object is put back."

Oliver nodded slowly and took the letter opener from his pocket, staring at it as his eyes welled with tears.

Ruthie had almost lost Jack once, and she too had felt the panic of being blocked temporarily from reentering a portal. But to have lived with those feelings for an entire life was unimaginable! The magic key had brought her so much excitement, but Ruthie was determined to prevent such heartache from happening to anyone else again. But how?

Then, from his other pocket, Oliver brought out the object that Ruthie had noted on his bookshelf. Now she saw that it was made of stone, about eight inches long. The color ranged from the palest minty white to deep shades of rich leaf green. Ornate swirls and fine details of floral patterns were engraved in the surface. "I'd better give you this too."

"What is it?" Ruthie asked.

Oliver shook his head. "I'm not sure. I took it from the Chinese room."

Mrs. McVittie answered the question. "It's called a *ruyi*, or scepter."

"Like a magician's scepter?" Jack said.

"More like a rabbit's foot. They are a traditional Chinese symbol of good luck. *Ruyi* roughly translates to 'as you wish.' This one looks quite old."

Oliver swallowed hard. "I suppose it might be . . . one of those animators. I'm sorry."

The room was silent for some time. Ruthie turned her gaze to the long walls of old books that led all the way to the window at the front of the shop. Hot beams of late-afternoon light illuminated the dust floating in the air. Ruthie wondered how much time it took a single speck to alight somewhere, how long it had traveled, and where it had started its journey.

Finally Oliver Brown asked, "Why didn't you bring her back?"

"She wanted us to find you first," Ruthie answered, not mentioning her suspicions that Rivy might opt to stay.

"Are you going to see her again?"

Ruthie nodded.

"She's waiting to hear if we found you," Jack answered.

"Could I . . . does the magic work for people like me?"

"We can make that happen," Ruthie said.

· · · 13 · · ·
A REASON TO LIE

"THINK ABOUT IT," JACK SAID, climbing up onto the bus. "Everything that's happened since 1977!"

It was the middle of Friday morning, past rush hour, so the bus wasn't jammed with riders. Ruthie found two empty seats next to each other.

"Elvis died," Jack began, "the first Star Wars movie came out, the first female astronaut went into space, personal computers started, there have been five presidents—including the first African American one, Barack Obama—a sheep was cloned, September eleventh happened, and we have the Internet, cell phones, video games, robots on Mars . . . there's lots more."

Ruthie agreed it was staggering to think how much had happened since Rivy disappeared. "I thought for sure she'd want to come back, but now I'm wondering . . . maybe she won't."

"Once she sees her brother, there's no telling how she'll feel. What time is he going to meet us?"

"We said one o'clock."

"That should give us enough time," Jack said.

First they planned to make a quick stop in the Chinese room, to put the scepter back. Ruthie tried hard not to let her imagination run wild, but she couldn't help herself; it might be a missing animator, trapping someone in China of long ago. They *had* to return it.

After that, they would find Rivy, to give her some advance warning about seeing her brother for the first time in nearly forty years. The last thing they wanted to do was surprise her, especially not in front of the Brownlow children.

Ruthie had also been feeling unsettled, not only since finding Mrs. Thorne's letter but also since hearing about what had happened to Rivy and Oliver. The Browns had found themselves in an unthinkable situation because they hadn't understood how the magic worked. Had she and Jack been lucky so far? Would their luck hold?

She must have been frowning because Jack asked, "Something wrong?"

"When we first found the key, I thought we would have exciting adventures only. But now . . . now it feels dangerous, like what are we going to run into today?"

"I know. It feels like we're walking through booby traps every time we go back in time," Jack said. "Too bad the key didn't come with instructions."

"I wonder what happened to the key after Oliver

dropped it," Ruthie pondered aloud. "He never saw it again. The next person to use it was Dr. Bell."

"The next person that we know of," Jack pointed out.

"Exactly. That drives me crazy; wondering who could have found it, and how it ended up back in the corridor for Dr. Bell to find."

"Yeah," Jack agreed.

"You know what else makes me crazy? If you'd been wearing shoes from 1867, Rivy never would have suspected that we were from this century and we might never have gotten to the truth."

Jack shook his head, looking at his feet. "It's always the shoes, isn't it?"

When they arrived at Gallery 11 they found it wasn't too busy except for a tour group and docent standing in front of the first European rooms, near the alcove. So Ruthie and Jack meandered to the American rooms, in the center of the gallery.

Standing in front of a row of California rooms, some of the last that Mrs. Thorne had created, Jack felt warmth coming from his pocket where he kept the key. He elbowed Ruthie and pointed to it. She understood.

"Is the scepter doing anything?" Jack asked.

Ruthie reached into her bag. The scepter was cold.

Jack moved down the wall, toward some rooms from the South. "The key's cooler here." He stepped back. "Warmer again. Weird."

The voice of the docent quieted, so Ruthie looked around the corner. "All clear. Let's go."

They let the key's magic work and in a few minutes they were in room E30, the Chinese room, the scepter safe in Ruthie's bag.

The room had no diorama, no garden or street scene around it. Instead they found a small opening in the framework that led them directly to a back corner of the room, not visible from the viewing window.

Ruthie could tell the room was already alive. The way the air moved across her skin, the subtle difference in the light and temperature, and scents that smelled strange told them that the room was a passage to another time. Ruthie exhaled deeply and thought how glad Oliver was going to be, knowing he hadn't trapped someone else by taking the jade scepter.

Now all they had to do was decide where to leave the scepter before going to find Rivy. Ruthie didn't remember seeing it in the catalogue, so it would be best to leave it in a drawer or another spot not visible to the public. Room E30 was more like a group of six interconnected spaces, each partially visible through walls that were solid on the bottom with open latticework on the top half. There was a lot to look at—every surface was carved or decorated with colorful inlays. Small stone carvings rested on black lacquer tables under silk tapestries.

"What's the time period for this room?" Jack asked.

"That's kind of a problem; the catalogue doesn't give a

time period. It only said the room is 'traditional' and that it could be from any time in a two-thousand-year period. Mrs. McVittie said the scepter might be thousands of years old."

"Sheesh. That's not very helpful. A thousand years would mean all the way back to before the time when Columbus sailed to America, you know—knights, the Dark Ages."

"I know." Ruthie subtracted another thousand years from the Dark Ages—back to the time of ancient Rome. She wasn't sure she'd want to visit that far back in time. Not without preparation anyway. "But it doesn't matter. We're just going to find a spot for the scepter, right?"

Jack didn't answer. He was studying a brush painting on one wall, with calligraphic characters running down the side.

"Can you read any of those?"

"We haven't gotten that far in class yet. We're still on the basics."

Ruthie led the way to a small sleeping area. A canopy bed that looked more like a carved wooden box with curtains was in the center. Instead of a mattress, Ruthie counted five thick folded blankets, stacked like pancakes, and made of colorfully patterned brocade. Two pairs of the smallest shoes she had ever seen were on the floor in front of the bed: one pale green with pink trim, the other black with white trim. They were smaller than Ruthie's hands in length. The toes were very pointy, so they didn't look at all like children's shoes—just for someone with very, very small feet. Ruthie reminded herself how tiny they must have been to Mrs. Thorne's craftsmen—unless, of course, they had been magically shrunk.

To one side they saw a dressing table with a silver hand mirror on it, and next to that a wooden chair with a metal bowl where the seat would be.

"Must be a toilet!" Ruthie said.

"I guess this room is from before plumbing," Jack surmised. "Hey—do you hear that? Voices!"

They followed the sounds to a door that was carved with cloud-like shapes and had a large brass knob. Jack put his ear to the door, holding his finger to his lips.

"I'll just take a quick look." Jack turned the shiny brass knob and eased the heavy door open wide enough for them to see out.

They saw an empty courtyard, enclosed by a high brick wall. "We'll be invisible for sure," Jack said. The voices came from beyond the courtyard.

They took a couple of steps.

The ground was covered in pebbles that made a soft crunching sound under their feet. Above the courtyard's wall they saw the tiled rooftops of other buildings, very close together. The voices had quieted for a moment and it was eerily silent. In the middle of the courtyard wall was a door with a black iron latch. They approached and Jack lifted the latch.

"Wait!" Ruthie felt prickles of caution rising. "We were just going to put the scepter back."

"Yeah, but . . . when are we going to get a chance to go to *China*?" Jack replied, and opened the door.

Outside was a narrow alleyway paved in cobblestones. The world out there smelled like dust, moist stones, and cooking aromas that Ruthie couldn't place. Jack stuck his head and shoulders out, looking first to the left and then to the right. He leaned a little farther when voices screamed out, and in an instant Jack was violently swept off his feet and carried away.

Ruthie pulled back instinctively, although no part of her had passed the doorway. A gang of eight or ten people had appeared out of nowhere, while Jack was looking in the opposite direction. Before they disappeared—with Jack—around the corner, Ruthie saw that they were big and muscular and had on matching dark clothes with tall leather boots. They wore hats that looked like fabric strips wrapped and wound in several layers.

She had no choice but to follow them.

As she rushed into the alley, the men were twenty feet or so in front of her, Jack's torso partially visible through the raging tangle of fists. Mrs. McVittie was right—the danger was real.

They turned a corner, and after passing a few doors, they pushed one open. Ruthie reached the door just as it slammed shut. She pushed hard but it was no use.

The men were shouting. She heard nothing coming from Jack.

Ruthie stood paralyzed, fear finally catching up to her.

Then she heard a faint cry: it was Jack, saying something—in Chinese! But the response came as mocking laughter. That shook the fear right out of her. There was no one else who could help. She raised her fist to knock.

"Wait!"

Astounded by hearing an English word, Ruthie spun around and came face to face with a Chinese boy her own height, dressed from boots to hat just like the mob that held Jack.

"I can help." He reached out a hand to hers and squeezed it. "Please. Out of the way."

Ruthie stepped aside, too stunned to do otherwise.

The Good Samaritan pounded on the door and shouted insistently until the door finally opened. A grizzled face appeared. They spoke a few sentences back and forth until the door opened wider, allowing them to enter. The boy grabbed Ruthie's arm and pulled her along. They were now in another courtyard, similar to the one they'd left.

Ruthie stifled a gasp when she saw Jack sitting on the ground, a purple hue blooming around one eye. A shouting match ensued between several members of the mob and the boy, who was gesticulating like a fiery politician.

Two of the men got in a shoving match, obviously in disagreement over what should be done. Finally, when the men were more consumed with arguing among themselves than with watching Jack, the boy helped Jack up. The threesome shot out the door and back to the alley.

"Are you all right?" Ruthie looked Jack over.

"We have no time! Come this way," the boy directed.

It crossed Ruthie's mind that they shouldn't follow, that they should go directly back to the courtyard that held the portal. But the boy's hand was already around Jack's arm, helping him along. They turned into an even narrower alleyway, and then through a door covered in peeling and chipped paint.

They entered a small, dark room. As Ruthie's eyes adjusted she saw that it was one of two rooms, partitioned just like the Thorne Rooms. Only there was no carved or glistening woodwork, just rough, cracked timbers with a dank smell in the air. A mat covered in tattered gray fabric lay in one corner.

"Who are you?" the boy demanded, his tone suddenly stern. "Don't make me regret saving you."

Jack had finally steadied. "I'm Jack Tucker."

"I'm Ruthie Stewart."

"Missionaries?"

"No. Just visiting," Ruthie answered.

"During the rebellion? Are you crazy? Where are your parents?"

Jack answered fast. "We got separated. Our dad is here to study the Chinese language."

"You tell the truth?"

"Why would we lie?" Jack responded.

The boy stared at Jack, then moved his piercing gaze to Ruthie.

"If you are lying . . ." He didn't finish; instead, he reached to take off his hat. Long hair tumbled out! "We all have reasons to lie!"

"You're . . . a girl!" Ruthie exclaimed.

The girl nodded. "They would never let a girl join."

"Join what?" Jack asked.

"The movement. The Righteous Harmony Society."

"Where'd you learn English?" Jack asked.

"My older sister works as a maid in the embassy. She teaches me."

"And what did you say to the men to let me go?"

"I told them I know you."

A gentle snore emanated from the other side of the partition.

"Shh. My grandfather sleeps."

"Do you live here?" Ruthie spoke softly.

"Yes."

"How old are you?" Ruthie asked.

The girl paused. "Eleven, I think."

"What's the movement?" Jack wanted to know. "And how long has it been going on?"

"It's to keep foreigners from running the country and forcing their religion on us. It started about a year ago. Some say we can't go into the twentieth century without being free."

"But why did you take the risk to help me?" Ruthie asked.

"I saw a girl like me who needed help." Then, with a hint of a smile, she said, "Oh, and my name is Ling. It means . . . *delicate*."

There was a drop of silence before all three laughed. Ling nodded toward Ruthie's messenger bag. "Do you have food in there?"

"Are you hungry?"

"I am always hungry!"

"I don't have any food . . . but . . ." Ruthie thought about the scepter, wondering if it would be of any value here. She reached into her bag and held it up. It still looked old, but not quite as old as it had when she placed it in her bag this morning. "I have this." She offered it to her.

Ling grinned. "A *ruyi*!" She took it in her palm, inspecting it. "A good one too!"

"Can you get money for it?" Ruthie asked.

"My sister can. Someone in the embassy would offer good money."

"Then you keep it." Ruthie closed the girl's fingers over it. "For saving Jack."

··· 14 ···

A STICKY SPOT

"WE'RE STILL OKAY ON TIME," Jack called up to Ruthie as she untangled the climbing ladder to hang from the ledge behind E4. Even though the hazardous detour into China felt epic, it had only taken about fifteen minutes. Jack took this moment to wander off down the short but dark corridor. Ruthie secured the ladder and was about to shrink when she heard him yell, "Help!"

She rushed around the corner.

It was too dark for Ruthie to see what had happened, but her first thought was *spider*—Jack had gotten caught in another web.

She could make out that his arms were waving to her, but the bottom half of him was frozen in mid-stride.

"What is it?"

"One of the rodent traps! My feet won't budge. I'm glued in place!"

Ruthie knelt down to get a look in the dim light.

The trap was a flat, glue-covered tray, about six by four inches, roughly the dimensions of a bathtub for tiny Jack. The surface of the black adhesive and the black plastic frame of the tray were nearly invisible against the dark floor. A couple of flies had landed on it, never to take off again.

"I'll just take my shoes off."

"But you're going to need your shoes. You can't walk around the museum without them."

She might as well have saved her breath because while she was talking Jack had bent over and lost his balance. He now sat awkwardly, thoroughly stuck. "Oops. At least my hands are free," he said sheepishly.

"Let me try to pull you off."

She grabbed hold of Jack's torso between her thumb and index finger and tried lifting him.

"Ow!" he shrieked. "You're going to break a rib!"

"Sorry."

It was no use; as she lifted him, the trap came up with him, and he felt stretched in two directions. "I think you're going to have to grow your way off of this."

"Okay. Let's do it."

Ruthie went back for the key and shrank. Then, tiny, she raced to Jack.

"Eww," Jack exclaimed as Ruthie got closer. A centipede had just slithered out from the shadowy corner and was now stuck. Though only five or so of its hundred legs

were on the glue, it couldn't free itself. It wriggled its hideous loose end. Ruthie could barely look.

"Get me off this thing!" Jack insisted, reaching out for Ruthie.

She took hold of his hand and tossed the key to the side, and the magic started. With a violent snap, the trap pulled off Jack's shoes and yanked at the seat of his pants. The tray rose and fell, the centipede flipping and flapping like the tail of a kite in a gust of wind. When they reached full size, the trap was only attached to the edge of Jack's right shoe. He reached down and, careful not to touch the creepy-crawly that was still frantically fighting the glue, he pulled the trap off. The glue stretched like taffy before it snapped free. When he took a step, the sole of his shoe was still a little sticky, as though it had chewing gum stuck to it, and made a slight noise as he walked.

"Sorry about that," he said.

"At least we got you unstuck. C'mon."

Ruthie grabbed Jack's hand and in no time they were scrambling up the ladder to E4.

The door was almost directly behind the folding screen, so they scooted in and slipped the period clothes they'd left there over their own. Ruthie peered around the screen to make sure they could walk across the room unseen.

Ruthie lifted the letter opener from her bag. "Let's put it on the secretary."

They proceeded across the room and set the sterling object on the desk. As soon as they did, it gave a little flash, and the magical bells rang out, the air itself sparkling with sound. The view through the window transformed from the dull flat colors of tempera paint to the rich greens of a living landscape. Fluttering leaves shimmered in the sunlight.

"Now the room will always be alive—even without the key and ring," Ruthie said with satisfaction.

It appeared to be late morning. Jack checked his watch and they exited to the patio. "I hope it doesn't take us too long to find Rivy."

"We should go to the house first and look for her there," Ruthie suggested.

"No need," they heard. It was Rivy, coming around the brick wall. "I'm here."

She grinned and gave them both hugs. Then she noticed Jack's eye.

Before she could ask what happened, he said, "I tripped and fell on my face. It doesn't hurt." He had developed a major shiner.

"How did you get here so fast?" Ruthie asked.

"I was around the corner with the children, doing our reading. I've come every day since we spoke . . . hoping that you would return," Rivy explained, her voice brimming with joy and relief. "I sensed the portal opening just moments ago. It was odd—I felt a slight tingle, a shiver almost. I came around and there it was!"

"And the Brownlow kids—can they see it?" Ruthie asked.

"It doesn't seem so. I have only a few moments, though, before I must get back to them. Did you . . . find Oliver?"

"We did!" Ruthie burst out.

"He wants to see you," Jack said.

"We came to tell you we're going to bring him here in a couple of hours. Can you be here then?" Ruthie asked.

"Of course!" Rivy clasped her hands together, her eyes beginning to glisten. "Is he . . . oh, never mind. I have so many questions—but I'll be able to ask him myself!"

She hugged them again. "I'd best be getting back now." Then she disappeared around the corner.

"That was easy," Ruthie said. They reentered the room, dropped the period clothes behind the screen, and were about to head for the corridor when Ruthie stopped. "I want to try something."

Ruthie still wanted to make sure she understood how the room had become animated without the letter opener when they had first entered several days ago. They experimented with various combinations. When they left the ring on the ledge in the corridor, the room stayed alive. When they left both the letter opener and the ring on the ledge, the room remained dead.

Jack replaced the ring with the key while Ruthie looked out the window. "Completely dead."

"Interesting," Jack commented. "It's like the key is some kind of master switch."

"It can make certain things animators," Ruthie said. "But not *everything*." She shuddered to think that she had considered leaving the ring with the Brownlow children at Belton House. Partnered with the key, the two objects became a temporary animator. Had they left the ring, separating it from the key, the portal would have closed. They too would have been captured by the past and might have never even understood why. The words from Mrs. Thorne's letter played once more like a recording in her head: *a most serious and dangerous matter.*

"Do you want to check anything else?"

She was about to say no when she heard two men speaking. She couldn't make out what they were saying but the voices were coming from the corridor!

"Quick!" Jack said, and rushed past her, out the door and into the framework.

Ruthie followed but as soon as her right foot passed from E4 into the framework, she felt a wind gust and her foot felt funny. She was beginning to grow! She instantly pulled back. Jack turned to see her standing in the doorway of the room.

"I'll grow—I'm not holding the key!" she whispered. The magic allowed her to be in the rooms or out in the past worlds without having the key. But once she left the room, even amid the wooden slats of the framework, she had to have the key with her or she would regrow. Ruthie could hardly believe her carelessness. She kept the door ajar so she could see Jack, but stood behind the folding screen, safely hidden from the viewing gallery.

Jack stood on the corridor side of the door. Through

the framework they eyed two men wearing maintenance workers' clothing. They had a flashlight aimed at the floor and they had just turned the corner, walking toward them.

The men stopped, right at E4.

"How many did you put out?" one man asked.

"Five or six," the other answered. "All empty."

One of them leaned against the ledge as he spoke—at the exact spot where Jack had left the key and letter opener.

"If he sees the letter opener, he'll see the key," Ruthie said as softly as she could. "You have to get them. I can't— I'll grow as soon as I'm on the ledge."

"I have an idea."

With the man's back still toward them and his body blocking the other man's view, Jack edged his right foot around the slat and out to the ledge. He reached the key and pressed his foot down on it. When he lifted his foot and pulled it back, the key had attached to the sticky spot on the sole of his shoe!

Ruthie grinned widely as her panic receded. Jack pulled the key from his shoe, then tiptoed over and handed it to her. She plunked it safely in her bag. Now she was able to go out into the framework with him. She pointed to the ledge again. Jack shook his head. The letter opener was too big and heavy for his gummed-up shoe to lift, and it was also farther away. Maybe their luck would hold and the men would leave without noticing it.

The men's conversation continued. They were on to the usual debate about the White Sox versus the Cubs.

The man closest to the ledge became more animated and gesticulated broadly as he spoke, lifting his elbow off the ledge several times, then returning it to almost the same place. But then he did it again, and his elbow came down on the letter opener.

"What . . . ?" He turned to find out what had poked his skin. With some difficulty he picked up the shiny miniature with his bulky fingers. "Hmmm. What's this?" He held it up and shone a flashlight on it. That was a good thing; adding the extra beam of light drowned out the magic glow emanating from the silver. "Looks like this belongs inside one of the rooms—not out here."

"Hey—what's that?" the other man said. Shining the flashlight on the ledge had also illuminated the ladder, which they hadn't noticed in the darkened space.

They inspected the ladder, looking at it and then at each other in disbelief.

"Maybe we have a prankster in the department," the first man said.

"We should see to it that the curator gets these."

The first man dropped the letter opener into his breast pocket and then bunched up the ladder, putting it into his pants pocket before going to the door.

"We have to get the letter opener back!" Ruthie whispered frantically, already whipping off the eighteenth-century clothes. Jack did the same.

"Don't worry. We have the ring and the key. Technically that's all we need."

Jack was right—*technically*. They would be able to reunite Oliver and his sister. But the *only* way to keep the portal open for Rivy permanently was with the letter opener. The ring only worked in combination with the key, and they couldn't leave the key in the room without also losing their ability to come and go—and shrink—as they pleased. Without a true animator in the room, Rivy would no longer have a choice about leaving her eighteenth-century life. She would have to come back with them or continue to be imprisoned in the past. Ruthie—or whoever had the key and the ring—would be her jailer, in control of the lock. It was an impossible situation.

They peeked around the wood slats and saw the door to Gallery 11 close. "Come on!" Jack said. They tossed the key to the floor and leapt into the air. The chase was on.

···15···
FUGITIVES

RUTHIE AND JACK JUMPED OFF the ledge and grew in midair, but they had to shrink again to exit the corridor. Waiting for a chance to grow, they peered under the door at the alcove. Lots of people had suddenly entered the gallery. They heard the workmen, but the sound of the men's voices diminished the farther from the alcove they walked.

"I can't hear them anymore," Ruthie whispered. "We're going to lose them!"

They didn't have the luxury of waiting for the perfect chance.

"Now!" Jack said, and they slid under and out. He grabbed Ruthie's hand and she dropped the key just as a young child turned around. The boy—about six—stood with his mouth gaping. Jack bent to scoop up the key while Ruthie put her finger to her lips, hoping that would keep him quiet.

"Sorry," Jack called as they dashed off.

Outside Gallery 11, the men were nowhere to be seen. Ruthie and Jack bounded up the stairs, trusting that was the path the men had taken.

On the main floor of the museum, Ruthie and Jack looked to the right, toward the Michigan Avenue lobby.

"I don't see them. We weren't that far behind them," Ruthie panted.

They headed left, going deeper into the museum.

"There they are," Jack said, resisting the impulse to point. They sped toward the men and then slowed to tail them at a good distance. They didn't want to draw their attention.

"How are we going to get the letter opener?" Jack asked.

"I'm thinking. All I know is we can't lose sight of them."

They entered a long hall-like gallery. They passed stone Buddhas and statues of other eastern deities, looking serene, perched on their platforms and pedestals.

The men stopped. Ruthie and Jack stopped as well. One of the men looked at his watch and said something. The two men parted, one continuing on to the eastern end of the museum, the other going toward the large plate glass doors of the new wing.

"Which guy has the opener?" Jack asked.

"I think it's that one." Ruthie pointed to the man going through the doors. "I bet he's leaving the building now."

"Then what?"

Ruthie shook her head—she hadn't the slightest idea.

They crossed the broad, sunlit lobby of the new wing. Instead of going to the exit, the man took a left at the coat check. Ruthie and Jack did the same.

The man walked past the coat check counter before disappearing through a door. Authorized Personnel Only, the sign read.

Jack stepped up to the counter. "What's through that door?"

The coat check attendant responded curtly, "It's off-limits."

Jack turned back to Ruthie and nodded toward a nearby bench, where they would be able to see anyone coming in or out of the coat check.

"What if he leaves the letter opener and the ladder somewhere in that off-limits area?" Ruthie worried.

"It's possible," Jack said.

"Yeah, but what if? Suppose we follow him out of the building and the opener's not in his pocket."

"Hey," Jack whispered, and elbowed Ruthie. "There he is!"

The man had come back out and was exiting the far end of the coat check carrying a lunch box. They jumped up from the bench and followed.

The man took the stairs up to the third floor, where an outdoor bridge delivered people to Millennium Park. The entrances and exits of the museum marked the limits of the magic's power to keep things shrunken. They would see the opener grow in his pocket—if he still had it.

The door closed behind them and the man stopped in his tracks. A small lump formed under the fabric of his shirt.

"Huh?" he mumbled with a start, and put his hand to his chest, the lump growing. In seconds the top half of the letter opener stuck out from his pocket.

The man pulled the full-size metal object from his pocket. The hot midday sunlight bounced off the polished blade and he blinked multiple times.

Without thinking or hesitating, Ruthie exclaimed, "You found it! Oh, thank you, thank you!"

"What—what's going on here?" the bewildered man stammered.

"I lost it in the museum!"

"It belonged to her grandma," Jack improvised. "Thanks!"

"I didn't ... it wasn't ..." was all the response he could muster, standing there scratching his head. "I'll be darned."

Ruthie put her hand out for it.

With a suspicious glare the man said, "Hold on, not so fast. I don't like the smell of this."

"It's true! I brought it here with me. It must have fallen out of my bag. Please give it back."

"It's hers!" Jack insisted.

Fumbling with his lunch box, he reached into his pocket and pulled out the wadded-up climbing ladder. "Is this yours too?"

"Never seen that before," Jack jumped in. "What is it?"

"Please!" Ruthie implored. "I need my letter opener."

By now several people had noticed the odd scene. The man gripped it even tighter.

"Prove it's yours," he demanded.

"The markings. I know the markings!"

"You do, do you?" the man asked skeptically.

"There's a lion, and a lion's head with a crown, and the number 925 stamped on the back," Ruthie answered.

He squinted to read the stamps and then looked at Ruthie. "And you just happened to bump into me?"

"I know—pretty lucky!" Jack responded.

"Where'd you lose it?"

"I'm not exactly sure," Ruthie sniffled. "The last time I know I had it was near the front staircase."

"And what about—you know—the size thing? How'd you do that?" he demanded.

"What size thing?" Jack asked.

"I don't know what you mean," Ruthie echoed, tipping her head to one side.

The man looked down at Ruthie as she wiped away a tear.

"No. This is going back to the curator. You can bring it up with her."

He started to walk away and Jack made a swipe for the opener, grabbing it before the man knew what happened. He darted off, the downward slope of the bridge giving him plenty of momentum.

The man glowered at Ruthie and she took off after Jack.

The man yelled something and started to chase them. Ruthie and Jack made it to the end of the bridge, down the short ramp, and onto a sidewalk. Going to the left would direct them to the giant bean sculpture and they might be able to get lost in the crowd. Or they could go straight, into the evergreen-enclosed prairie garden, and find cover in the tall grasses. They hesitated for a split second and then dove for the maze-like garden. They sped along the pathways.

From somewhere behind them the man yelled, "Where are you?" Ruthie's heart pounded; this was no game of tag.

Since they couldn't see him, they figured he couldn't see them either. They were right about that until they crossed a small bridge over a man-made creek that split the garden in half. The bridge raised them just enough for him to catch a glimpse of their heads.

"Aha!" he shouted. He was closer than they had reckoned.

"Quick!" Jack pivoted to the right. "I know how we can lose him."

Several yards ahead were stairs leading out of the park and to Monroe Street. They tore down them, taking multiple steps at a time. Jack darted to the right and Ruthie followed.

There, not twenty feet away, was an entrance to the underground parking garage with three huge levels of endless parking. They ran into the small lobby, past the pay machines, and down a stairwell to the lowest level, not slowing at all. They dodged down a row of cars and ducked between a parked SUV and the wall. Ruthie thought her lungs would burst. They huddled and tried to quiet their breathing. When he got back his wind, Jack peeked out.

After a minute or two, the man came out of the stairwell, panting hard. He stood, looking all around. Then he put his hands on his knees, as though he'd finished a marathon, and it appeared he had given up. He turned around and pushed the button for the elevator. He got on and the door closed.

"I can't believe we did that," Ruthie rasped. "Let's wait for a few minutes."

"Okay." Jack gave her the letter opener and she put it in her bag.

Ruthie startled at the sound of footsteps. They froze as the echoing clip-clop of shoes on concrete grew louder. But it was only a woman far down the row, walking to her car.

"Do you know your way around?" Ruthie asked.

"I think there's an exit on Randolph Street. If we keep going north we should find it." Jack took his phone from his pocket. He made a few taps, pulling up his compass app. "That way."

They passed row after row of cars. Ruthie couldn't help but think of all the others on the levels above them, and on top of that, the weight of Millennium Park itself, with its gardens and trees, sculptures and band shell. Her chest felt tight and her eyes played tricks on her, as though the space were closing in.

Ruthie thought she should have been used to this by now; after all, she'd tunneled through the ductwork under and over Gallery 11. But she wasn't. The exhaust fans, with their constant loud rumble, did nothing to quell the stagnant heat.

Ruthie felt like a fugitive. But she was determined not to let anyone gain control of the animator. Having it meant freedom for Rivy.

In another five minutes they spied the sign for the Randolph Street exit. Ruthie felt the space expand around her, but not from magic—from relief!

They rode the elevator to the sidewalk, where the white vertical lines of the Standard Oil building across Randolph Street pointed upward to the blue sky. There was no man chasing them, the letter opener was safe in her bag, and Ruthie breathed normally for the first time in an hour. They sank down onto a nearby bench in the shade to cool down.

"Next problem," Jack said. "How do we get Oliver—and us—to the rooms without the ladder?"

Ruthie thought for a minute. "I have an idea. Where's the nearest store with school supplies?" she asked.

"Monroe and Wabash," Jack answered. "Why?"

"Remember when Oliver told us how he and Rivy had

climbed?" Ruthie asked, jumping up from the bench. "They used pushpins. We could do that!"

They had to find a store and get back to meet Oliver at the museum steps at one o'clock. Ruthie led the way as they weaved through the pedestrians crossing Michigan Avenue. Jack was correct: there was a big pharmacy at the corner.

They charged in and ran down the aisles until they found the right one.

"Here," Jack said, finding the pushpins first.

He grabbed a package and they headed for the checkout. The line wasn't too long. They paid the bill and were back out on the sidewalk. Jack checked his watch: twelve forty-five. They arrived at the steps of the Art Institute and waited for Oliver by the bronze lion on the north end of the steps.

There were lots of people walking up and down the steps as well as sitting on them. Ruthie overheard a couple near them speaking in French. A day-camp group of seven-year-olds made their way up the steps.

"Do you think he'll be on time?" Ruthie asked.

"Probably. You saw how neat his desk was. I bet he's never late."

"Uh-oh," Ruthie gasped. She thought she saw the maintenance man approaching the stairs. They ducked behind the lion, peering between the legs, but it was a false alarm.

On edge now, they continued to scout the crowd. "Here he comes," Ruthie said, and stood up. Oliver Brown was in the crosswalk. They ran down and greeted him at the base of the steps.

Oliver noticed Jack's black eye. "What happened to you?"

Jack brushed off the question by saying, "Tripped. No big deal."

"I was afraid you wouldn't be here," Oliver admitted nervously. "I thought maybe I had imagined our meeting."

"It was real," Jack reassured him.

Ruthie thought how odd it was to see a grown man biting his lip like a small child. In fact, there was something boyish about him even in the suit and tie.

"Are you ready?" she asked.

"Ready as I'll ever be. Are you sure this is going to work?"

"Positive," Jack said. "Let's go."

···16···
THE CHOICE

THE ART INSTITUTE IS FREE for kids, but Oliver had to buy a ticket. He also had to leave his briefcase in the coat check. After he did, they went directly down to Gallery 11. Ruthie kept a careful eye out for the maintenance man, but for some reason she felt more secure walking with a responsible-looking grown-up.

Oliver tensed as they approached the entrance; his pace slowed and he stiffened, like his legs were resisting.

Entering the gallery, he took a deep breath and gazed around. "What do we do now?"

Jack answered in a low voice. "We stay near that alcove over there, and when the coast is clear, I'll hand the key to Ruthie. She'll take your hand. Just hold on and don't let go."

Oliver nodded.

Finally it happened; Jack slapped the key into Ruthie's

left palm, she clasped Oliver's hand with her right, and the magic spread like electricity through the three of them. The breeze blew and the space rushed up and away in every direction. Ruthie had never noticed before how the carpet loops seemed to grow like mushrooms in time-lapse photography. When the process stopped, Jack pulled Oliver down and guided him under the door.

"You okay?" Jack asked on the other side.

Oliver nodded uncertainly.

"I'll have to get big again, to set up the climbing system," Ruthie explained.

When she dropped the key and regrew, Oliver lost his balance momentarily as he witnessed Ruthie and the key enlarge on the floor in front of him.

"The room that'll take us to your sister is right up there," Jack said, pointing to the glow coming from E4.

"I can't believe it's going to happen. It's been forty years. We may not even recognize each other." Oliver sounded worried.

Ruthie opened the box of pins and started pushing them into the wall, two staggered rows all the way up to the ledge. She looked at that juncture, wondering how they would manage it: the ledge jutted out from the wall, like the eave of a roof. She stuck a pin on the topside of the ledge and then foraged through her bag for some kind of string. She found a broken hair elastic, which she tied to the top pushpin and the one she stuck into the ledge.

Like a climber's rope, it would guide them up and over the protrusion.

"I could lift the two of you if you don't want to climb," Ruthie offered.

"No special treatment for me," Oliver said. "I'll climb if you climb."

"Let's do this!" Jack said.

Ruthie picked up the key. Oliver watched again in amazement as both she and the key shrank.

Jack went first, reaching up to hold on to one of the gigantic pushpins and lifting first one foot and then the other. Each pin was about as big in circumference as a roll of paper towels but not quite as long. They were easy to stand on but somewhat harder to grab hold of. Oliver followed, and Ruthie brought up the rear. They all got the hang of it fast, and Ruthie admired Rivy's invention.

"Piece of cake," Jack said after he climbed up a bit.

Oliver agreed. "I remember doing this."

"This is helpful," Jack called down to Ruthie as he approached the jog at the ledge and used her giant elastic. They were so small and light, the elastic gave barely at all.

By the time Ruthie reached the top, Jack was already showing Oliver the wooden framework and pointing out the door that led into E4, the Belton House room.

"Would you like to put this back?" Ruthie asked, bringing the letter opener from her bag.

"Look at it!" Oliver said. The sparkles and glints

brightened their faces in the shadowy space of the framework.

"The magic's warming up," Jack explained.

Oliver accepted the letter opener. Ruthie cracked the door and took a look inside. The room appeared dead, as she expected. "Jack's got the ring in his pocket. As long as we keep it separate from the key, they won't animate the room. You'll do it with the opener."

Oliver nodded.

"Let's go," she said.

They went in, and a look of recognition spread across Oliver's face. Ruthie led him across the tapestry rug to the tall secretary. "We don't have a lot of time. People will be coming by," she urged.

Almost like a sleepwalker, he approached. He laid the letter opener on the writing surface, next to a silver candlestick. As soon as he did, the sound of the magic began, softly at first, then building until it filled the space, before subsiding.

"What was that?" he asked.

"That was the sound of the room coming alive," Jack said.

Sure enough, a cloud passed in front of the sun outside the room, softly dimming the light that filtered through the window and onto the desk. A moment later it brightened as the cloud blew away on a breeze.

"We need to move on," Ruthie said, but just as she started toward the door to the patio, she stopped. "Listen."

It was the sound of the grandfather clock that stood in the corner, next to the door. It was ticking.

"Cool," Jack said.

The air out on the patio felt good against her skin after the heavy heat of the city. Every time they'd gone back to the eighteenth century, Ruthie had noticed how fresh it was. After all, they were breathing air that had not yet been filled with fumes from factory smokestacks, car and truck exhaust, or even the black plumes from train engines. She had time to ponder this; Rivy was nowhere to be seen.

"But she told you she'd come?" Oliver asked for the second time.

"Yes. Just this morning."

"She'll show up," Jack added with confidence. "Belton House is right over there." He pointed it out to Oliver. "Let's wait in the spot where she sits with the kids."

Since none of them had donned eighteenth-century clothes, they didn't want to wander too far from the portal. Oliver and Ruthie sat on the small bench, and Jack sat on the ground. Birds chirped in the trees. Oliver checked his watch and wiped his brow. His eyes darted from Belton House, up on the rise, back to the portal.

At last a figure appeared in the distance.

Ruthie jumped up. "There she is!"

Oliver stood as well, but slowly, as though a great weight rested on his shoulders.

"Oliver?" Rivy whispered, her voice tight. She looked

almost as nervous as her brother. "Oliver!" Her hand went to her mouth and tears flooded her eyes. She reached out to touch his cheek, but then she took a step forward and threw her arms around him.

Slowly his arms rose to embrace her, as if the gesture were new to him. Ruthie and Jack eased back. Ruthie blinked away tears herself, and a lump grew in her throat, which she gave up trying to swallow away.

Rivy and Oliver sat on the bench together. "I wasn't expecting you to be . . . so grown-up!" Rivy said.

Ruthie and Jack leaned against a tree, watching them in silence but far enough away to give them some privacy. Ruthie saw more of a resemblance as they talked.

After a while Jack nudged Ruthie and said softly, "I wonder if my phone camera will work." He took his phone from his pocket and walked over to them. "Want a picture?"

"What is that?" Rivy asked.

"It's a phone," Oliver answered.

"And a camera," Jack added.

Her eyes were wide in disbelief. "The future really did come!"

Jack snapped a picture and showed it to her.

"There's so much you're going to have to learn about when we get you home," Oliver said.

A slight frown formed on Rivy's face. "But I . . . ," she began, and turned away. "I don't know if I can."

"Of course you can!" Oliver turned to Ruthie and Jack. "Right? The magic will bring her back home."

"Yes. It will," Ruthie responded. But she understood what Rivy was saying before it dawned on Oliver.

"No, Oliver. I know the magic will bring me back. But . . ."

"But what?"

"It's been a long time. I have a life here. As much as I longed to see you and understand what happened all those years ago, I don't think I can leave the children. Not now, at least. They've been my family . . . this has been my world for almost all of my life!"

Oliver's back became rigid once more, his expression dulled. His pain crossed the air right to Ruthie's heart.

"When Ruthie and Jack found me several days ago, I thought my wishes had been fulfilled," Rivy began to explain. "I had dreamed that someday the door would reappear and that my old life would be delivered to me."

"It has been!" Oliver contended.

Rivy gently cupped her hand to his cheek again. "Don't you see? My old life is just that. *The old one.* I have a new life here."

"I can't believe this! What about me?" Oliver said, standing up and stomping his foot. "You left me once!" he shouted, and slumped back down on the bench. He remained silent for a moment before speaking again. "I'm sorry. You didn't leave me. I understand that now. . . . I left you."

"You were only a little boy. I forgive you. But I'm sorry too. I was responsible for you. It was also my fault."

"No, it wasn't!" Ruthie broke in. "It wasn't anyone's fault. None of us knows exactly what this magic power can do! It's dangerous," she said, hearing herself once again repeating the word that Mrs. Thorne had used.

"Ruthie's right," Jack agreed.

"Rivy, remember what we told you about animators in the rooms? You should know we put it back," Ruthie explained.

"What was it?"

"A letter opener," Ruthie answered.

"I took it when I ran off," Oliver confessed. "I thought it was a dagger."

"So that means the portal will be open for you from now on," Ruthie reminded her. "You could come back if you change your mind. Whenever you want."

A lightness entered Rivy's eyes and her brow softened. She lifted a linen handkerchief to her eyes, then turned to Ruthie and Jack. "I'm profoundly grateful that you found Oliver and brought him to me." She hugged Oliver once more and then followed them to the portal.

"Are you sure?" Oliver asked her.

"The children are waiting for their afternoon lessons. They would miss me; they wouldn't know what happened to me. We can't have that happen—you know what that felt like," she replied.

"I understand." He gave her a long embrace.

Ruthie and Jack hugged Rivy goodbye, and the three of them walked through the door and into room E4. They crossed the room on their way to the corridor.

"Hang on," Jack said, and dashed back to the secretary. Barely lifting the letter opener from the writing surface, he slid it into one of the drawers. "It's been gone from the room so long," he explained, "I don't want anyone to notice it and decide it doesn't belong. And I really don't want that maintenance guy to see it. Look," he said, pointing through the window at Rivy walking back to Belton House. "It's still alive out there."

"Good thinking," Ruthie said. A subtle quake vibrated across her nerves as she thought of the consequences had Jack not taken this one simple precaution. She couldn't bear to think of what else she might have overlooked.

"I have to get my briefcase," Oliver said in the lobby. Ruthie and Jack waited near the front doors while he stood in line.

"That was . . . I don't know . . . *surprising*?" Ruthie said.

"I know," Jack agreed. "It's sort of like your birthday. Like there's some present that you want really badly. And you get it and you're happy, but the best part was waiting for it."

"I guess. But does that work when the thing you want is a person?"

Jack considered this. "At least they both know they weren't deserted by the other one. Neither one has to feel bad about that anymore."

"That's huge," Ruthie agreed.

Jack shrugged. "I think they both have to get used to how their lives just changed."

Oliver returned from the checkroom. His face looked more relaxed. "I haven't properly thanked you for what you've done."

"We were glad to help," Ruthie said.

"And I see now that my sister may never be able to come back. I can't leave my life, so I shouldn't have expected Becky to be able to leave hers. I suppose I could think of it like she's living overseas. People have family members all over the world," he said, mentally putting the pieces in order, just like all the elements on his desk. "But knowing what happened and that we love each other is the most important thing."

Ruthie understood what he meant. She wasn't sure what to say but was glad that Oliver accepted Rivy's choice.

Walking down the steps of the museum, Ruthie stopped. "I almost forgot!" She looked in her bag and found the two rings. "These are yours."

Oliver slipped the Brownlow family ring onto his pinkie and looked satisfied. Holding the mood ring in his palm, he chuckled. "Funny—when I was a kid I thought this was the really great one!"

"Jack! Your eye! What happened?" Mrs. McVittie exclaimed. She listened in silence from her desk chair while Ruthie and Jack explained what happened. "You're not going to like what I have to say."

"Tell us," Ruthie said.

"Of course, I'm very proud of you for what you did for Oliver and his sister. But I think it is time to stop."

"Stop what?" Jack asked.

"Exploring the rooms. Going back in time. I've been worried about your safety. First, Ruthie nearly being stranded in another century." She turned to Jack. "And now your eye—you could have been seriously injured. Or worse!"

"But Mrs. McVittie—" Jack began.

She shook her head.

Ruthie didn't say anything, but she knew Mrs. McVittie had a point. Things had gotten dangerous—she'd thought so herself. Their magical visits to the Thorne Rooms were no longer simply an exciting secret adventure—there were very real and frightening forces at work with the magic. Mrs. Thorne's letter stated as much.

The next several days dragged. As they worked, a silent chill floated in the shop air. Mrs. McVittie had put her foot down—they were to promise her they would never use the key again.

Ruthie felt as though there'd been a cosmic shake-up, bits and pieces falling randomly and nothing landing where she expected. Rivy—who belonged in the twenty-first century—had to stay with the Brownlow children in the eighteenth. Even though Ruthie had felt satisfaction from ensuring that Rivy was no longer a prisoner in the past and made the choice to stay at Belton House of her own free will, that feeling was whisked away when she thought of Mrs. Thorne's letter. Ruthie couldn't imagine how they would ever fulfill Mrs. Thorne's wish of putting the key where it belonged, in its "looking-glass box." The responsibility weighed on her like the hot and heavy Chicago air.

Everything had gotten so complicated. Having the key now felt like a burden to Ruthie. What should they do with this piece of magic? To whom should they return it? It was such an old mystery, and most of the people involved were long gone. If only she had been able to meet Mrs. Thorne, to ask her what to do. She wished she could go back in time and talk to . . .

"Jack!"

· · · 17 : · ·
MONTJOIE

Dear Mrs. McVittie,

We hope you won't be too angry with us. You are right, the magic is dangerous, and we know that now. But we have to figure out what to do with the key. So we are going back to the rooms one more time for answers. We are going to look for Mrs. Thorne. We promise to be careful and hope you understand.

Love,

Ruthie and Jack

Ruthie and Jack slipped the letter under the door of Mrs. McVittie's shop early Thursday morning.

The night before, they had finally put the pieces together. They could not be certain they had it right; it was like doing a jigsaw puzzle without having a picture of the final product. But the letter and address—Montjoie, Santa Barbara, California—reminded Ruthie of something she'd read in the catalogue. The entry for room A35 (a California room from 1935–40) noted that Mrs. Thorne knew about Santa Barbara because many of her friends spent the winter there, away from the harsh cold of Chicago.

Ruthie reminded Jack about what had happened on Monday in front of room A35: the key had flashed when they'd stood near that room. She did an Internet search and discovered that Mrs. Thorne in fact had a winter house in Santa Barbara, designed by the same architect who had helped her plan many of the miniature rooms. The house even had a name, Montjoie. She printed the address and a map.

Ruthie had a hunch that A35 would lead them to Mrs. Thorne.

They made their way into the corridor and up to the room, then peeked inside through a door painted in soft green with shimmering gold. It was a living room with a high, beamed ceiling, stucco walls, and dark wood furniture. Another door opened into a back room, and one more led to a stairway going up. The warm glow of the California sun shone through a glass patio door, bouncing off the glazed tile floor. The room was alive!

Hoping to determine what animated the room—and looking for clues that would lead them to Mrs. Thorne— they picked up any item that looked truly old. Finally, on a table near the patio door, Jack found it: a small wood figurine of an Indian goddess in a flowing gown, standing on a lotus petal. He picked it up, and as soon as he did, they heard the faraway bells—like the sound was playing backward. The light in the room became almost imperceptibly bluer, colder. Ruthie hadn't exactly noticed the slight scent of honeysuckle until it evaporated and the air in the room went stale.

Jack set the small statue down, and the room came back to life.

Ruthie opened the patio door and took a few steps out into the sunshine, but Jack had his eye on a fat gold-embossed book. He picked it up and flipped it open to the middle. It turned out to be an old naturalist's book, filled with illustrations of plants and animals, describing their habitats and behaviors. Some of the creatures were fanciful and odd. The tome was just the kind of thing Jack could have spent hours looking over. But he had to stop and put it down because he heard voices nearby in the gallery.

Backing up a few steps and pivoting at the same time, Jack was moving too quickly and tripped over his own feet. To save himself from falling he grabbed one of the yellow curtain panels hanging on either side of the door. But the curtain came down, rod and all! The entire treatment landed in a heap.

There was no way to fix it quickly and the voices were getting closer. The only option was to drag the entire pile, curtains and rod, to the patio.

"What happened?" Ruthie asked when she saw Jack hauling the felled curtain.

"I tripped but I got out just in time," he answered. "I can't believe I broke part of a Thorne Room."

"It'll be okay," she said, feigning calm, though this rattled her even more. She helped him shove everything out of sight behind some plantings.

A low stucco wall enclosed the patio. Not too far off they saw the town of Santa Barbara and the deep blue of the Pacific Ocean beyond. In the other direction rose the mountains, dotted with houses. One of them, Ruthie hoped, was Mrs. Thorne's.

They took a good look at the map before they left the patio, then found a couple of street signs to locate their position. They estimated that they were a little over one very winding mile from Montjoie. They left the invisibility of the patio and walked briskly uphill.

The air was warm but not hot and the sweet smell of honeysuckle was more intense outside. Ruthie saw why: lush vines of it climbed and hung over fences in most yards. A few old-fashioned cars were parked here and there and palm trees swayed overhead.

The gravel road twisted and turned back on itself, like a mountain path. After about forty minutes a vehicle passed by them—a pickup truck with big, bulky fenders. The silver chrome of the bumpers and front grill sparkled in the sunlight, and the spare tire was plunked right on the side. The back contained gardening tools and a dog. The pooch gave them a friendly yip and the driver slowed and smiled at them.

"Need a lift?"

Ruthie and Jack thought of their promise to Mrs. McVittie to be extra careful. Ruthie answered, "No, thanks. But do you know how far the Thorne house is?"

"You're almost there—top of the rise, just follow me. I'm on my way to work."

"I can't believe it! We're actually going to meet her!" Ruthie said to Jack as the truck pulled ahead of them.

"We don't know for sure that she's there," Jack reminded Ruthie. Because of the California climate, they didn't know what time of year they'd entered. Maybe Mrs. Thorne was back in Chicago.

They arrived at the top of the hill. Two white pillars supported a wrought-iron gate with a big *M* in the middle. The gardener waited for them by the gate. "Are you here to see Mrs. Thorne's granddaughter?"

Ruthie answered truthfully, "No, we're here to talk to Mrs. Thorne about her miniature rooms in Chicago."

"Come with me and I'll ask if she's available."

"He's so nice," Ruthie whispered to Jack, feeling more hopeful with every step.

The driveway turned and in front of them they saw the house. It was tall and stately, painted cheery yellow and trimmed in white. The gardener brought them to the front door.

"Wait here," he said, pointing at his dirty work boots. "I'll go round back."

Ruthie's heart thumped in her throat. "I'm nervous."

"Me too," Jack admitted.

The door opened. They had seen a few pictures of Mrs. Thorne: the oil painting of her as a young woman hanging in Gallery 11, and a black and white one in the catalogue when she was nearly eighty years old. The woman who opened the door was neither young nor old. She wore a belted dress of pale blue with a white collar. Her hair was short and softly curled.

The woman smiled politely and said, "Yes?"

"I'm Ruthie Stewart and this is Jack Tucker, and we've come from Chicago—"

"A *really* long trip," Jack interjected.

"Yes, an *extremely* long trip, to talk to Mrs. Thorne about her miniature rooms."

The smile vanished and the woman peered into their faces intently. She took in their clothes, their shoes, Ruthie's messenger bag.

"I am Narcissa Thorne." Her voice cracked almost imperceptibly. "Come in, please."

She turned and they followed her inside into a living room with huge windows looking out to the ocean.

"Please have a seat." Mrs. Thorne motioned to a sofa while she sat in a chair next to it. "I believe that you have

indeed come an *extremely* long way to find me," she said, making a point of repeating Ruthie's word. "Do you know what year it is?"

"Nineteen thirty-nine?" Jack responded.

She took a deep breath and shook her head. "Nineteen forty-one. I was so hoping someone would come— sooner. But now the worst has happened: two children have found me."

Ruthie looked at Jack, and he looked back at her. In 1941 the rooms had been finished only the year before, and they were touring the country. Mrs. Thorne had written the letter just two years earlier. But they had not stumbled upon the letter for nearly three-quarters of a century!

"So . . . you were expecting someone? Who?" Jack asked.

"I don't know precisely. I hoped it would be someone I know. Anyone from my studio who had access to the key."

Ruthie chose her words carefully. "Do you know why we're here?"

"You have the key," she answered. "And what year did you come from?"

Jack answered, and added, "Late June."

"Oh, dear! It's worse than I could have imagined. All those years!" She had been sitting up straight, with the same perfect posture she had in the oil painting, but with this news she fell back in the chair, her hands raised to her temples.

"Yes," Ruthie began, "we found it last February—"

"Please, stop. We have to be very, very careful."

"Why?" Ruthie asked.

"Since you have the key and you are here in front of me, it means you understand about the time travel. Did you come through room A35?"

"Yes," Ruthie answered.

"And this is not your first time travel?"

"That's right."

"And you must have found my letter?"

"Yes," Ruthie said. "Hidden in a vase in one of the European rooms."

"In miniature?" she asked, astounded.

"Yes."

Mrs. Thorne shook her head. "I left it in the studio."

"We don't know who took—or stole—the key in the first place," Ruthie said.

"Yeah, I just found it on the ground in the corridor a few months ago," Jack added.

"But . . . ," Ruthie began, but then stopped, having remembered that the rooms hadn't even been installed in the Art Institute yet. "You can't possibly even know about the corridor."

"That's correct. And even if you knew who took the key from my studio, I would not want you to tell me. We can't do anything that will change the course of the rooms' history—for your sake." She looked at them, her mouth tight. "Do you understand what I'm saying?"

"We do," Ruthie nodded. They had altered the course of history once before, writing Jack out of existence, and Ruthie had desperately raced against time to correct their blunder and bring him back. Some small misstep now could have similar terrifying consequences!

"I didn't know—until now—if whoever took the key knew of its magic. I was deliberately vague about that in my letter, hoping someone just took it as a piece of jewelry." She paused and shook her head. "Too much time has passed since the key left my possession. Many lives could be impacted by what we do today—including yours! You mustn't tell me anything today that will change my behavior in the future. Even if you think it might help someone."

There was a deep silence in the room except for the far-off sound of the ocean breaking on the beach.

"In your letter, you said you had a vault. Could we put the key there?" Ruthie asked.

"No. I thought I could—if someone returned it right away. But now . . . you must take it with you, don't you see?"

And then it sank in. They couldn't leave it here. If they did, it would change what had already happened. Mrs. Thorne would have the key from 1941 onward, causing a chain reaction of events. Jack would never have found the key, they would not have helped Sophie or Louisa, Kendra's family history would be completely different, Dora might still be stealing from the rooms, and the little boy at the fair would have been killed by the tram. Ruthie didn't want to undo all the good they had done! Her brain felt like it was being turned inside out as she tried to solve this puzzle.

"I understand your dilemma. I wrote the letter hoping that whoever had taken the key would return it immediately, before so much . . . so much history had occurred," Mrs. Thorne said gently. "I've thought long and hard about it. Let me tell you what I know about the key."

The archives had it partially correct. Ruthie and Jack had read that one of Mrs. Thorne's craftsmen, A. W. Pederson, had found the key in an old dollhouse from Denmark. What they didn't know—and what Mrs. Thorne proceeded to tell them—was that she had been searching for the key for years. She had learned of its existence from other collectors in her travels around the world. She was determined to find it, to know if the legend about its magical powers was true. It became her obsession and fueled her passion for miniatures.

Ruthie and Jack sat rapt. Narcissa Thorne was able to tell them many things that had happened up until 1939. She felt it unsafe to mention anything past that date, when she had lost possession of the key. It took a lot of concentration for Ruthie and Jack to speak as carefully. Once Ruthie even put her hand over Jack's mouth to stop him.

"But I learned quickly that the power was dangerous and had to be used rarely, if at all. I hope you two have learned the same lesson."

"We've been really lucky," Jack said.

"I have a question," Ruthie began, the puzzle still missing some pieces. "We found some other objects—a metal slave tag, a ring, and a coin—that were also magic. Do you know anything about them?"

"There is an old man in a shop in Paris—I will not tell you his name—who has kept track of as many of these objects as possible. He calls them talismans, and they facilitate time travel in various ways. The key works in my miniatures and can sometimes activate other antique objects. There are other portals, but he would never tell me where they are."

Ruthie wanted to speak up and mention the animators, but she remained silent.

"It has been his life's work," Mrs. Thorne continued, "to keep a list and to collect them if he can. I don't know about the tag and the coin. But I believe you. No one knows how many objects have been imbued with the power. Some—like the key—seem to be more powerful than others. Those of us who have hunted down these talismans have learned the magic is ancient. It comes from the special metal alloy. The key becomes magic when mixed with one other element."

She stopped.

"What?" Jack was not going to let her leave it at that. "What other element?"

"A spell," Narcissa Thorne answered.

··· 18 ···
HOPE OF
FUTURE YEARS

"A SPELL?" RUTHIE AND JACK asked simultaneously.

"We heard Duchess Christina mention a spell," Jack blurted out.

Mrs. Thorne rose from her chair. "Come. Let me show you something important."

They followed her out of the room and into a paneled library. She walked to a set of bookcases and put her hand on a brass handle that appeared to be on a drawer between two shelves. She pulled hard, and instead of a drawer opening, the entire section of bookcase moved, revealing a hidden vault behind it.

"Awesome!" Jack exclaimed.

Set in the wall was the circular dial of a walk-in safe made of a steely-colored metal. Mrs. Thorne dialed the combination and opened the substantial door. She lifted a single item from the top of a file cabinet.

"The key belongs in this."

It was a box, about four inches square and covered in mirrored glass. Old glass, to be sure, the kind that has gray streaks breaking through the bottom layer and clouding the mirror. Mrs. Thorne opened it and they saw the interior was also mirrored. A crimson pillow lay inside.

Ruthie felt heat from her messenger bag. She opened it and the key flashed.

"This is called a looking-glass box. Somehow—who knows how or in what century—the key was separated from the box. It was my goal to reunite them. And I did, until the key went missing from my studio."

"Why did you want to reunite them?" Jack asked.

"To stop the magic," she said. "When I first heard of this legendary key, I thought time travel would be an extraordinary adventure. I know better now. Time travel is too dangerous, and the key can so easily fall into the wrong hands. That it disappeared on my watch has weighed heavily on me."

She lifted the pillow to show them that words had been etched into the old glass underneath. It was quite difficult to read.

"That is the spell."

"What's the spell supposed to do?" Jack asked.

"When the key is in the box and the spell is spoken, it should both turn on and turn off the magic."

"Do you know if it works?" Ruthie asked.

"My friend in Paris insisted that it would. But I wasn't able to make it work when I had them together in my studio. Perhaps the conditions weren't right. Or perhaps the key and the box have been separated too long. And because I didn't know if the person who took the key was aware of its powers, I thought it best to bring the box here."

Taking a long look, they were able to make out the words and read the spell.

TALL WILL BE SMALL
AND
BREAK
THE TIES OF TIME
UNTIL
WHAT WASN'T
IS
WHAT ISN'T
AND
THEN IS NOW
NOW IS THEN
AND
SMALL WILL BE TALL

"It's like a really confusing poem," Ruthie said. "Or a riddle."

"Should we try it now?" Jack asked.

"No!" Ruthie exclaimed.

"Ruthie is right; it's too risky. Since I wasn't able to make it work in my studio, I think there may be something I don't understand about it. If someone from my studio had come—and sooner—I might have taken the chance. But I won't with you. Suppose we were unable to rekindle the magic? I could not live with myself knowing that I had trapped you in 1941."

"If we can't leave the key here, maybe we could bring it through the portal, just far enough to say the spell. The box won't disappear until we are far from the rooms," Ruthie suggested.

"It won't work. Objects brought through the portals are illusory, without substance. You might be able to see the box and even hold it in your hands for a short while, but it would not be completely of substance and it won't have its power. I am certain of this law of the magic." Mrs. Thorne set the box back in the vault.

"That explains a lot," Jack said, thinking of all the things they had brought through the portals that had disappeared once they left the museum.

"What *can* we do with the key, then?" Ruthie worried.

Mrs. Thorne shook her head, sighing. They left the vault and she closed the secret door. "I think you must go. Put the key in the safest place you can think of."

Walking out into the perfect oceanside paradise made it seem as though nothing at all could be wrong in the world. Mrs. Thorne offered to take them back to the portal of A35. "I'll just have my driver get the car."

"Wait!" Ruthie said. They had heard about her driver from Isabelle, and Ruthie wanted to be sure this driver was not the same man. "Is this your driver from Chicago?"

Very carefully Mrs. Thorne answered, "No. This is my California driver only."

Ruthie exhaled. "That should be fine."

When the car came around from the carriage house, they were once again startled to see an old car looking so new. This one was a pale yellow convertible and had the brand name DeSoto spelled in shiny chrome. The three climbed in and headed down the winding road to the intersection where Ruthie and Jack had arrived.

Because Mrs. Thorne was not magically in Santa Barbara of 1941, she couldn't see the stucco wall and the patio garden, as Ruthie and Jack could. What she saw was simply an empty lot, with scruffy trees and overgrown vines. Nevertheless, she got out of the car with them and told the driver to take a spin around the block.

"It's right here," Jack said, approaching the opening in the wall.

"If you take my hand, I will see it," Mrs. Thorne said.

Ruthie clasped hands with Narcissa Thorne, who immediately said, "Ah! There it is!"

They walked onto the patio, the glass doors to the room straight ahead.

"Do you want to look in?" Ruthie asked.

"I think that would be unwise. Seeing the door is enough."

Still holding Mrs. Thorne's hand, Ruthie leaned in to see if the coast was clear for them to enter. "It's safe to . . . Wait, something's happening—"

Her sentence was interrupted by violent shaking and rumbling. At first they thought it was an earthquake, but this vibration came from every direction, not just under their feet. They were thrown in the air—air that had become pitch-black in an instant. They were thrust away from where they'd been standing, first rising up, and then tumbling through space. In just seconds they landed hard and the sunlight returned.

They found themselves sitting on the sidewalk, Ruthie and Mrs. Thorne no longer holding hands.

"What was that?" Jack said.

"Are you okay?" Ruthie said to Mrs. Thorne.

"I believe so." She stood and dusted off her dress. "You'd better go back immediately."

"Mrs. Thorne," Jack said with a gulp, for he saw it first: the low stucco wall and patio had disappeared, and all that remained was an overgrown empty lot. "I don't think we can."

They waited over an hour for the portal to reappear, while Mrs. Thorne's driver patiently sat in the car. The breeze blew from the ocean, carrying not a single tinkling of magic bells on it.

"What time is it, Jack?" Ruthie asked.

His watch still ticked off 2014 time. "Almost two o'clock."

"No, it's almost three o'clock," Mrs. Thorne corrected, checking hers.

"The time out here isn't always the same as our time," Jack explained.

Mrs. Thorne responded simply with a raised eyebrow.

They had no idea why this was happening. Could someone have taken the animator from the room? That seemed impossible. They still had the key. Ruthie was feeling sick to her stomach from anger at herself. She knew better than anyone that the portals could close, but she had ignored the risk.

"One thing perplexes me," Mrs. Thorne said. "Just before things went black, I noticed what looked like the room's gold curtain on the ground near the door, off to one side. Did either of you notice that?"

"Uh-oh," Jack said. "Mrs. Thorne, just before we left, I tripped and pulled the curtain down," he confessed. "But I dragged it out of sight so no one would notice."

"What would that have to do with anything?" Ruthie asked.

"That may explain what happened," Mrs. Thorne answered. "It wasn't magic that shut the portal—*it was maintenance!* Someone removed the room so they could repair it."

"It did sort of look like the room was rushing away from me," Ruthie recalled.

"You mean, they took it right out of the wall?" Jack asked.

"Yes—the dioramas and all. We designed them so they could be removed that way."

"When will they put it back?" Ruthie asked, trying not to get hysterical.

"It could be days. Unless they decide the room needs thorough conservation—in that case, it could be weeks."

"Oh, man. This is all my fault," Jack said.

"There's no sense waiting here," Mrs. Thorne said.

"But . . . but . . ." Ruthie didn't know what she had meant to say. She felt just like she did when the portal had closed on her before, in eighteenth-century England. She didn't want to take her eyes off the spot where it would—where it *must*—reappear. It was the only way back home!

Or was it?

"Jack! Remember when we went to Belton House? After we met Freddy?"

"Yeah, why?"

"We realized that maybe we could go in one room and out another if they were from the same time!"

"Oh, right! I figured out how long it would take us on horseback!"

"Exactly! *A37!* It's the same time!" Ruthie nearly screamed.

"That's right," Mrs. Thorne confirmed. "But it's not here in Santa Barbara."

"I know—it's in San Francisco. Do you know where the portal is?"

"It's an apartment belonging to a friend. But it would take at least six hours to drive there."

"It's Thursday, right?" Jack asked. "We have till eight o'clock, when the museum closes."

The timing was tight. They might get there after the Art Institute closed. Ruthie thought about how much trouble they would be in if they returned to the closed museum. But she didn't care—they would be home! Mrs. McVittie would be waiting for them at the shop and her parents would be expecting her home for dinner.

"Get in the car!" Mrs. Thorne said, grinning widely. "We'll go to the airfield. I have a small plane."

They didn't have to drive far. The airfield consisted of a runway, a large hangar where the planes were kept, and a smaller building where passengers gathered. Inside, Ruthie saw a couple of vending machines that sold Coca-Cola and cigarettes, and a waiting area with several chairs. A somber voice came from a radio. Mrs. Thorne went straight to a man in a gray-blue pilot's jumpsuit sitting behind a desk.

"Narcissa! What can I do for you?"

"Jim, these are two friends of mine from Chicago. We thought we'd fly up to San Francisco," she said as matter-of-factly as if they were grabbing a taxi for a ride up the street.

"Great day for flying," he replied. "I'll rev her up and

have you in the air in twenty minutes." He headed out the door to the airplane hangar.

As simple as that, Ruthie thought.

"We'll board as soon as it's on the tarmac," Mrs. Thorne explained. "Let's have a seat while we wait."

"Hey, listen," Jack said.

All three became aware of the voice on the radio.

"It's Mr. Churchill," Mrs. Thorne said, "the prime minister of England."

His voice was distinctive and rumbling—Ruthie had never heard anything quite like it.

"What month is this?" Jack asked.

"February," Mrs. Thorne answered. "Europe is at war."

Ruthie had thought she couldn't feel any more anxious than she already was, but the prime minister's words sent chills up and down her spine: "We must all be prepared to meet gas attacks and parachute attacks with practiced skill. In order to win the war, Hitler must destroy Great Britain."

"I can hardly bear to think how the British will survive." Mrs. Thorne looked at Ruthie and Jack. "Of course, you know how it all turns out. . . ."

The prime minister then quoted from a poem:

> *"Humanity with all its fears*
> *With all the hope of future years*
> *Is hanging breathless on thy fate."*

Though Ruthie knew better, it seemed as if he were talking directly to the three of them. He finished in a deep growl, "Give us the tools and we will finish the job!" Then the radio went silent except for the crackly static of dead air before the announcer came back on.

Mrs. Thorne gazed out the window with sorrowful eyes. "There is so much about the future I want to know—about the war and the world, about my rooms . . . but I will have to wait and live it."

Shortly they heard the chop-chop of the propeller slicing the air, and the plane came into view out the window. A single propeller spun on the front, and the wings extended from the top. Jack jumped up, eager for the ride, but Ruthie thought the airplane looked awfully tiny, like a toy come to life.

The plane came to a stop, although the motor and propeller were still running. They followed Mrs. Thorne out onto the tarmac and another airport employee jogged over to them to open the plane's door and help them aboard.

"It won't be quite so loud inside!" Mrs. Thorne shouted over the din of the propeller, gesturing for Ruthie and Jack to climb in first.

It was a tight squeeze; neither Ruthie nor Jack could stand up straight. There were two seats at the front, one for the pilot and another next to him. In the back, a downward-sloping center aisle separated four seats. The

plane narrowed to a small windowless cargo area in the tail end.

The three took their places, and the pilot turned back to them. "Buckle up and we'll be on our way."

The motor roared and Ruthie felt all the bumps on the runway as they taxied to the end for takeoff. The pilot turned the aircraft, accelerating quickly, and in seconds the nose lifted and they were off the ground.

Ruthie looked out to her left and saw nothing but blue: the azure of the ocean growing deeper to the inky horizon, meeting the cloudless sky. Out the right-side windows she saw the mountains, which shrank as the plane climbed higher.

The flight took a little less than two hours; for the first thirty minutes, Ruthie was distracted by the novelty and the view. But once she got used to it, worries nudged back into her mind. Would this plan work? As far as Ruthie and Jack knew, no one had ever tried it before. And as for Mrs. Thorne, Ruthie sensed that the woman to whom they had come for answers didn't know either.

Ruthie closed her eyes. In her mind appeared images of her home, her parents, Mrs. McVittie, Jack's mom. Everyone and everything she loved were waiting for her seventy-five years in the future, perhaps lost forever in the messy maze of years that time travel created.

She opened her eyes. The plane continued along the California coast, the sunlight reflecting off the ocean like a mirror, which made her think about the beautiful yet strange box in Mrs. Thorne's vault.

And the riddle-like spell etched into the glass—was it real magic at all? The key and the other magic items she and Jack had come across—*talismans*, the mystery man in Paris called them—needed no spells or incantations to work. The key only needed to be in Ruthie's hands and near the rooms. Perhaps the old man was wrong and this mirrored box was nothing more than an antique red herring.

She opened her messenger bag and took out a pen and a small notebook she always carried. "Mrs. Thorne!" Ruthie shouted, and tapped her in the seat in front of her.

"Yes, dear?"

"Do you know the spell? Can you write it down for me?" Ruthie offered the notebook and pen.

"I know it by heart." Mrs. Thorne jotted down the words and handed the notebook back.

Ruthie looked at Mrs. Thorne's perfect penmanship. She read the words over and over, committing them to memory.

"I see San Francisco. We're almost there," Jack announced. He looked at his watch. "We're doing okay."

···19···
THE SPELL

AFTER A HALF-HOUR DRIVE FROM the airport, a taxi dropped Ruthie, Jack, and Mrs. Thorne at the doorstep to a building that looked very new compared to the surrounding structures. The lines were simple and smooth, with tall narrow windows. Ruthie remembered the catalogue had said A37 was a penthouse. She looked up and counted about ten stories, where she saw the low wall of a balcony. The last orange and gold of sunset streaked the edge of the sky, while the deep sapphire of evening spread.

In the lobby Mrs. Thorne gave a uniformed desk attendant the name of her friend. He announced them by phone and then directed them to the elevator.

"What time is it, Jack?" Ruthie asked.

"Five forty-five."

"No, six forty-five," the attendant interjected.

"Thanks." Jack waved his hand.

The ding of the floors rang out ten times as they rode the elevator. The door slid open and a butler greeted them. He welcomed Mrs. Thorne and told them that the owner—her friend—would be home shortly. He ushered them into the living room, leaving them to wait.

"Good. It will be easier to get you back without having to make up an explanation," Mrs. Thorne said, exhaling.

"So how do we find the portal?" Jack asked, turning 360 degrees. He looked behind a curtain and checked the walls for hidden doorways.

"It should be out there," Mrs. Thorne said, pointing to the balcony.

Ruthie headed to the tall glass door and walked outside. The deepening twilight reminded her that they were running out of time to get home before the Art Institute closed. In the distance the two towers of the Golden Gate Bridge caught the last rays from the sun and looked as though they were on fire. *Wait a minute—what did the catalogue say about the bridge? You could see it from the balcony. We must be on the right track*, Ruthie told herself.

Jack and Mrs. Thorne appeared on the balcony.

"It has to be out here," Ruthie said, looking out over the city as lights began to twinkle from buildings. "See? This is nearly the same view."

"And the view from A37 is nighttime, right?" Jack reminded them. "It's almost dark."

"Right!"

"How far does the balcony go?"

"If we can find the exact view . . ." Ruthie headed to the left, where the balcony wrapped around the penthouse like an up-in-the-air backyard. "There it is!" she shrieked as Jack and Mrs. Thorne came around the corner.

"Are you sure?" Mrs. Thorne asked. "I only see the stone of the building."

"That proves it's the portal," Ruthie said. "You can't see it!"

Ruthie and Jack saw an arrangement of patio furniture that was identical to the miniature furniture. The low wall of the balcony enclosed a small area around a glass door—most certainly leading to A37. Home was just through that door!

Ruthie held out her hand for Mrs. Thorne to clasp so she could see the portal. "Can you see it now?"

"Yes!"

Jack, already at the threshold looking in, announced, "It's A37, all right!"

Ruthie turned to Mrs. Thorne and saw a glittery sheen of tears forming in her eyes. She blinked them away.

"You two are very brave. Thank you for trying to return the key to me."

"Thank *you*, Mrs. Thorne," Ruthie said. "For helping us . . . and for making the rooms!"

"I had an idea on the plane ride. I'm not sure it will work," Mrs. Thorne began. "Can you give me an address where I can send something to you?"

"Sure. But how?" Jack replied.

"Leave that to me."

Ruthie took a page from her notebook and wrote down Mrs. McVittie's shop address.

Jack looked at his watch again. "We should go. Well, I guess this is goodbye." He put his hand out to shake Mrs. Thorne's. She pulled him into a hug instead, and then Ruthie. They walked her out to the low wall that defined the edge of the portal and watched as she returned to 1941.

Ruthie felt a bittersweet twinge run through her as they made their way across the room, back to the corridor and twenty-first-century Chicago. This was likely the last time she and Jack would use the key. Ruthie felt both relief and sadness.

She stopped and took Jack's arm. "Look, just look," she said, their backs to the giant door to Gallery 11. They lingered a moment, remembering all the adventures that the dark passage had led them to.

In the gallery, after they'd grown big again, they looked around the corner at the wall that held A35. Just as Mrs. Thorne had guessed, a black curtain was draped in front of its spot, and a sign stated "Temporarily Removed for Maintenance."

Ruthie didn't say a word as they raced through the museum, now full size, on their way to the exit, but one horrible thought popped into her head: *Is there any chance at all that we came back to the wrong time? Everything looks the same. But what if it's a different day? Or month?*

Jack obviously had no such fears. Instead he was already checking his phone, texting Mrs. McVittie, who had sent multiple messages.

Ah, of course! She too checked her phone, which showed the date. The messages from Mrs. McVittie were all from today. *The real today.* The one Ruthie expected. And boy, was Mrs. McVittie worried and angry. But that was just fine!

"Looks like we're in big trouble!" Jack said, smiling anyway.

The following Wednesday—July 1—was another hot Chicago day, so Ruthie and Jack were glad to be working in the storeroom. They arrived bright and early, and they hadn't been working very long before they heard someone come into the shop.

"I'm looking for a Miss Ruthie Stewart and a Mr. Jack Tucker," a man's voice said.

"May I ask why?" Mrs. McVittie responded.

"It's a legal matter."

Ruthie looked at Jack and whispered, "Are we in some kind of trouble?"

Jack shrugged. "Beats me."

They peeked through the storeroom door in time to see an elderly man give Mrs. McVittie his business card.

"I represent the estate of Narcissa Thorne."

On hearing that, the two nearly stepped on each other as they rushed to the front room.

"I'm Ruthie and this is Jack."

The man was taken aback. "I was expecting you to be . . . much older." He put a hand forward to shake theirs. "This shouldn't take long."

He opened his briefcase and took out a letter. "Narcissa Thorne died in 1966, but long before that she had written her will. Her estate was fairly sizable, the bulk of it going to her relatives and some charitable trusts. But she had left one boxed item and this letter, to be delivered to this address, on this very date. We at the law firm found this very unusual, but it was all legal. We don't know what is in the box, nor the content of the letter. But as the lawyer for her estate, this is the last act I must execute." He handed the letter to Ruthie and Jack.

> To Ruthie Stewart and Jack Tucker
> (age eleven or thereabouts),
>
> In recognition of your courage and your deep commitment to the virtue of responsibility, I leave this one item to you, with deep gratitude. You will know what to do with it. I hope it has reached you as you have reached me.
>
> Good luck in your future. Enjoy living your life every day, one at a time, in order.
>
> Ever yours,
> Narcissa Thorne
> February 15, 1941

"What item?" Jack asked.

Ruthie thought she knew.

The lawyer took a cardboard box from his briefcase. It was a sturdy one, a little smaller than a shoebox, sealed with heavy tape. The only writing on it was in Mrs. Thorne's distinctive handwriting—*To be opened by Ruthie Stewart and Jack Tucker ONLY.*

"I hope you all know what this is about, because it's been a mystery to all of us at the firm for many years!"

"Why don't you open it?" Mrs. McVittie suggested. She handed Ruthie a pair of scissors from her desk.

Ruthie carefully cut through the tape and lifted the flaps. She saw rumpled tissue paper within. But through the paper a glint caught her eye, a reflection of light on old glass.

"Oh, right!" Jack said as Ruthie lifted the mirrored box out.

"What a lovely antique," Mrs. McVittie exclaimed.

"Would you care to tell me why Mrs. Thorne left it to you two?" the lawyer asked.

"We could tell you," Jack said, "but you'd never believe us in a million years!"

"Well, wills are filled with all kinds of unusual requests," the lawyer said with a shrug. He closed up his briefcase and headed to the door. "Stay cool today."

"The key belongs in this box," Ruthie explained to Mrs. McVittie as soon as the door closed.

They had planned to have Mrs. McVittie put the key in a safe-deposit box, but in the meantime it was hidden in one of her desk drawers. She took it out now.

The key flashed wildly as Ruthie lifted it and brought her hand near the box. She paused, unsure of what would happen. Then she noticed a note amid the crumpled tissue. She read it, her jaw dropping. Jack looked over her shoulder and read along.

> Dear Ruthie,
>
> I consulted my friend in Paris. He explained something I hadn't known when you came to see me: according to legend, the spell must be recited by a young girl, no older than Duchess Christina.
>
> So, you see, it had to be you!
>
> Narcissa Thorne

"Cool!" Jack said, patting her back as though she'd won the lottery. Then he lifted the little velvet pillow for Mrs. McVittie to see the words. "This is the spell."

"I can't quite make it out."

"I memorized it," Ruthie announced, while Mrs. McVittie tried to read the fancy script.

"Tell me!"

Ruthie hesitated.

"Go ahead," Jack said. "It's not supposed to do anything unless the key is in the box, remember?"

Ruthie recited the spell once.

"Now let's put the key in," Jack suggested. He put the key on the pillow and placed them both in the box. "Say it again."

Ruthie spoke the magic words. The key's flickers intensified, bouncing off the sides of the box. The flashing quieted to a gentle pulse.

"What is the spell supposed to do?" Mrs. McVittie asked.

"It's supposed to turn the magic on and off."

"Doesn't it seem like something more should have happened?" Ruthie said, relieved but disappointed. "It looks like the key still has its power."

"Mrs. Thorne said she couldn't get it to work in her studio," Jack reminded them. "At least the two things are back together. That's what Mrs. Thorne wanted."

"But she also wanted the magic turned off," Ruthie pointed out. "She thought it was too dangerous."

Ruthie looked at the box one more time and reached out to close the lid. As she did so, she felt the warmth that signaled the magic. It shot through her fingertips like a hot shiver. The words of the spell came to her, first as she had memorized them but then jumping around in her head, mixing like a marching band changing formation. Something was happening, but it wasn't shrinking or time travel. Rather, a vague dizziness came over her, an inside-out, upside-down, and backward kind of sensation. Backward . . . *backward!*

"Ruthie?" Mrs. McVittie said as she saw her teeter a bit.

Ruthie pulled her hand back. "I've got it!"

Jack turned around. "Got what?"

"The spell! We've been saying it one way, the way it's written. We *assumed* that was the only way."

"And?"

"The box is a clue. The mirrors! I kept wondering why it had so many mirrors. The spell can be read two ways, like a mirror reverses things!"

"You think if you say the spell the other way—like backward—the magic will be turned off?"

"I know it sounds crazy. . . ."

"Not at all," Mrs. McVittie said. "I think it sounds thoroughly plausible."

"Try it!"

"Here goes." Ruthie opened the box. She began to recite the centuries-old words, in the opposite order:

SMALL WILL BE TALL
AND
NOW IS THEN
THEN IS NOW
AND
WHAT ISN'T
IS
WHAT WASN'T
UNTIL
THE TIES OF TIME

BREAK
AND
TALL WILL BE SMALL

The breeze they had until now experienced only in the corridor suddenly swept around them in the shop, and the most dazzling light show they had ever seen erupted from the box. The white radiance was so bright that Ruthie had to close her eyes until it transformed into prismatic shots of crystalline color, rainbow beams bouncing off in every direction. The walls of the dusty old shop reverberated as the magic bells sounded all around them, brighter and louder than ever before, a thousand tiny chimes ringing in unison.

And then the spectacle stopped. The key no longer pulsed; not even a whisper of light came off it. It looked like a tarnished antique.

"Brilliant!" Jack exclaimed.

"Mrs. Thorne would be pleased!" Mrs. McVittie said.

"I know the chances are small," Ruthie said, "but what if someday someone gets hold of the box and key and reads the spell? The magic will continue."

"Mrs. Thorne thought it should be stopped for good," Jack added.

"I have an idea." Mrs. McVittie rose from her chair and went to a small box of antique jewelry, rummaged through, and found a silver chain—nothing too fancy, but a good one. She then removed the key from the pillow and slipped it onto the chain.

"You keep it. Wear it." Mrs. McVittie put it on Ruthie, hooking the clasp at the back of her neck.

"Me?"

"Good idea." Jack nodded his approval. "I think Mrs. Thorne wanted you to have it. She even said it: 'It had to be you.'"

Ruthie felt the solid weight of the key on her skin, just under the dent between her collarbones. The metal was cold, the way it should be. She would wear it always, as a symbol of the important job that had been meant for her and which she had seen through to the end. And it would be a reminder of the magical adventures that she had shared with her best friend. To all the world the key would look like a pretty piece of jewelry, and no one would ever guess the magic it had unlocked.

Room E4, English Drawing Room of the Late Jacobean Period. The letter opener that Oliver took from the room is in one of the drawers in the secretary desk.

AUTHOR'S NOTE

MY STORY IS FICTION, BUT my characters visit real locations and moments in history, so I want to be as accurate as possible in describing these times and places. I had a lot of fun digging into the historical eras that Ruthie and Jack travel to in this book.

I have long been interested in the seventeenth and eighteenth centuries, a span of time called the Age of Enlightenment and considered (in the West) to be the birth of the modern era. The ring dial, although a small and humble device, represents that age to me, when people explored the world and invented tools that they believed would bring them objective truth through accurate measurement.

I was excited when I learned that Narcissa Thorne based one of her rooms on a period room in the Metropolitan Museum of Art in New York City. In fact, one of the reasons she started re-creating period rooms in miniature was in response to the Met's installations. She realized that a museum can only give so much space to full-size re-creations, but if they were done in one-twelfth scale, there would be room for many more. She already loved miniatures, but this gave her a reason to start her ambitious project. The Wentworth Room offered Ruthie and Jack the perfect way to stumble into New York City on the eve of the United States' entry into World War II, and witness the contrast of the idealism expressed at the World's Fair.

The 1939 World's Fair featured amazing new structures that reflected "The World of Tomorrow."

Early in the story Jack comes across a newspaper advertisement for an exhibition called "The Treasures of Tutankhamun." It was considered the first blockbuster museum exhibition and set all kinds of attendance records. It has been reprised many times, with new objects added, and has toured the world. (I saw it in Chicago in my freshman year of college. It coincided with the first Star Wars movie—both franchises are still going strong!)

King Tut's mask was part of the "Treasures of Tutankhamun" exhibition.

During Ruthie and Jack's brief visit to China at the turn of the twentieth century, they meet a young girl who was part of the Righteous Harmony Society movement. This was an uprising by citizens who believed foreigners had too much influence in China and wanted them out. Sometimes the group was called the Righteous and Harmonious Fists, because they had limited weaponry and had to rely on their physical strength and boxing skills—their movement is often referred to as the Boxer Rebellion.

In researching Mrs. Thorne, I went to Santa Barbara and found her house there, Montjoie. It is a private residence so I was not able to tour it, but from the outside it is grand and elegant, like so many of the Thorne Rooms. It was designed by the architect Edwin Clark, who designed her residence outside of Chicago and drew the plans for many of the miniature rooms. He was also the architect for many notable buildings in Chicago, including the Brookfield Zoo.

When I was thinking about the spell that would activate the magic in Duchess Christina's key, I came across a wonderful book by Marilyn Singer called *Mirror Mirror*. In it, she retells famous fairy tales in a form of poetry she calls reversos—the same words read backward reverse the meaning of the story. Her invention is very clever and deceptively simple. I love that I was able to respond to her work with a creation of my own—much like I did with Mrs. Thorne's creations, like Mrs. Thorne did with the Metropolitan Museum's, and maybe like you will do with mine.

RESOURCES

I LEARNED MUCH OF MY world history through the study of art history. A good beginning book for younger readers is *The Art Book for Children* by the Editors of Phaidon Press.

For older students, Khan Academy has excellent tutorials on a wide range of artists and eras: khanacademy.org /humanities/art-history.

The ring dial worked using latitude. Longitude was a more difficult measurement, and ways to determine it occupied many scientists in the eighteenth century. For younger readers who want to learn about this (and the importance of timepieces like the ring dial), read *Sea Clocks: The Story of Longitude* by Louise Borden, illustrated by Erik Blegvad.

And for older readers and teachers: *Longitude: The True Story of a Lone Genius Who Solved the Greatest Scientific Problem of His Time* by Dava Sobel.

There are several versions of the catalogue that

accompanied the many King Tut exhibitions as they have traveled over the years. A good book with an overview of the excavation of the tomb is *The Complete Tutankhamun: The King, the Tomb, the Royal Treasure* by Nicholas Reeves.

National Geographic has interesting information about the mummy of King Tut at ngm.nationalgeographic.com /2005/06/king-tut/williams-text.

There are many great books about the 1939 World's Fair. For beautiful photographs from the period, try *The New York World's Fair 1939/1940 in 155 Photographs by Richard Wurts and Others.*

And for a fun look at the fair, and to see what "educational" films were like (and how they bordered on being propaganda!), watch *The Middleton Family at the New York World's Fair:* archive.org/details/middleton_family_worlds_fair_1939.

To see the room from the Wentworth house that inspired Mrs. Thorne, go to the Met's website at metmuseum .org/Collections/search-the-collections/9790.

And to see all of the Thorne Rooms, go to the website of the Art Institute of Chicago at artic.edu/aic/collections /thorne.

Or check out the catalogue of the rooms: *Miniature Rooms: The Thorne Rooms at the Art Institute of Chicago.*

ACKNOWLEDGMENTS

WRITING IS A LOT LIKE gardening; seeds germinate, flowers bloom, weeds grow, and great effort is necessary. From working in my garden I've learned that wild honeysuckle, no matter how lush and sweet-smelling, has to be hacked away periodically. Shana Corey, my brilliant editor at Random House, has been my steady guide in the pruning and sculpting of the manuscripts. She graciously tells me how lovely a certain passage may be, and then gently points out that—like those beautiful plants in the wrong place—it must go. I will be forever grateful to her for her letters, corrections, questions, and enthusiasm.

I would like to thank the other wonderful folks at Random House who have worked on this series: Nicole de las Heras for her art direction—the books are beautiful in every way thanks to her—and Rachel Feld, Alison Kolani, Casey Lloyd, Mary Van Akin, Lisa

McClatchey, Lisa Nadel, Paula Sadler, Adrienne Wain-
traub, and the extraordinary sales team all have my sin-
cere thanks.

I am extraordinarily lucky that Greg Call signed on as
my illustrator. He brought Ruthie and Jack to life and created the visual presence of magic on the pages of all four
books. I can't imagine a better artist for the job.

Thank you to Mican Morgan at the Art Institute, who
has answered my questions but more importantly has been
patient with kids who come into the museum, fiddling
with locks and looking for the secret corridor! I'd also
like to thank her crew of docents who have energetically
embraced the books.

My friends and family have been with me all the way
on the project; my sister, Emilie Nichols, who listens and
laughs with me; Anne Slichter, my friend and go-to reader;
Masha Block, for saving me in numerous ways; my son,
Henry, for his good cheer and general helpfulness; my
daughter Maya, for her amazing analytic skills, and my
daughter Noni, who can conjure up her ten-year-old self.
We added two new family members over the course of the
series, Dave Segal (who married Maya) and Eric Brueck-
ner (who married Noni); thank you both for joining in on
the fun.

I also owe a debt of gratitude to my agent, Gail Hoch-
man. First, for connecting me to Shana. But above all,
Gail is a nurturer, tough and direct, yet smart and caring.
Marianne Merola, who works with Gail, has been a tireless

champion of the books (and made it possible for me to receive fan mail from Japan, Poland, Israel, and more!). My thanks go to all who work at Brandt and Hochman.

And last but most of all, I give thanks to my husband, Jonathan Fineberg. He knows firsthand the rhythms of a writer's life and is my rock, my friend, my love.

ABOUT THE AUTHOR

MARIANNE MALONE is an artist, a former art teacher, and the mother of three grown children. Marianne says, "Writing is a kind of conjuring. I write because I believe in the magic of art to transport. I hope my readers will be moved by my stories in the same way that I was moved as a young girl (and a grown one!) by Mrs. Thorne's creations."

Marianne lives in Urbana, Illinois, with her husband, Jonathan Fineberg. For teacher guides (including Common Core tie-ins) and more, visit mariannemalone.com.

ABOUT THE ILLUSTRATOR

GREG CALL began his career in advertising before becoming a full-time illustrator. He works in various media for clients in music, entertainment, and publishing. Greg lives with his wife and two children in northwestern Montana, where he sculpts, paints, illustrates, and (deadlines permitting) enjoys the great outdoors with his family.